The A CLUB

The blogs of
ABI GOODENOUGH

LION
Children's Books

Text copyright © 2006 Vince Cross
This edition copyright © 2006 Lion Hudson

The moral rights of the author
have been asserted

A Lion Children's Book
an imprint of
Lion Hudson plc
Mayfield House, 256 Banbury Road,
Oxford OX2 7DH, England
www.lionhudson.com
ISBN-13: 978-0-7459-6019-7
ISBN-10: 0-7459-6019-7

First edition 2006
10 9 8 7 6 5 4 3 2 1 0

A catalogue record for this book is available
from the British Library

Typeset in 10/14 Garamond ITC
Printed and bound in Great Britain
by Cox and Wyman Ltd, Reading

What do you think?

Is the future more like an endless road or a huge painting?

If the future's like a road, then it stretches out in front of us, and we're just looking through the windows of the car as we whizz along. Stuff happens, and there's nothing we can do about it.

If your vote's for the massive painting, then it's us making the stuff happen. We're all up there together like Michelangelo and his merry men, slapping on our tags, talking to each other, swapping ideas, never finishing. The future's down to you and me.

I really want to know which is true.

Fact.

I, Abi Goodenough, am a very busy person.

Let's start with work. School. By my count, that's 195 days a year eight thirty to four with half an hour lunch break every day except Monday ('to minimise vandalism of the school fabric'). And while we're talking lunch, I make my own. Salads. I would *never* trust the school canteen.

195 days, that is, minus any sick note time. Though illness is virtually unknown in the Goodenough household. We just pretend we're not sick, and wait to be sent home when we've finally puked over the school library carpet. Well, I *was* only eight. But these

things stay with you. Total time off last year: two days. *Really* bad period: one day. Strange spots which *might* have been something infectious: one day.

Then there's travelling time. (Approx. one hour a day however you do it, car, bus, on foot. Slightly less if Mum's driving.) That's an *extra eight days a year*! What a thought! What a waste!

Homework. Unpredictable factor and therefore a potential source of major stress. Might be two hours a night. Might be ten minutes. My point is, how do you know when enough's good enough? (*'Good enough is never enough for a Goodenough.'* Yes, thank you, Dad. Now shut up!)

Monday night. Tap class six till seven. Stupid time, but what can you do? I like tap.

Tuesday. Basketball team practice after school in the sports hall. Five o'clock finish. Possibly. But I don't mind. As sports go, basketball's cool. And maybe later in the term I'll get to be team captain. Which would be nice. Never been captain of anything before.

Wednesday. County Youth Choir. Yawn, yawn… Fauré's *Requiem*… yawn, yawn. Supposed to stop at 8 p.m.. Usually on its last croak at about half past. After-hours singing courtesy of Jemima aka Droopy Drawers aka our esteemed conductor, Miss Everard. Can't find her music, can't remember what we did last week, can't cope with anything less than total perfection, has us practising standing up and sitting down for hours on end. Completely hopeless!

Thursday. 'Tomorrow's People', i.e. the church youth group. Six to seven. Don't laugh. Not quite as bad as it sounds. Sounds complete pants though. Must tell Jana and co. to bin the name. And they're surprised kids aren't beating the door down?

Friday. Clash of the Titans. Youth theatre at the local college, seven till nine. *And* church choir/music group at much the same time. Can't win. One or the other's always in a strop when I stand them up.

Saturday morning. Jazz class at dance school nine till ten. Then change in fifteen seconds max. Grab fiddle. Run up road to County Music School trailing tights, deodorant, music. Try to look amazed everyone's so early for rehearsal. Lasts till noon.

Saturday p.m.. So when did you *think* I get to do the weekend homework?

Sunday. Church most of the morning. Then Sunday Lunch. No avoiding *that* particular date with danger. Because we're so Christian and wonderful, might be anyone there from Gran to the local dossers, and likely to go on a bit too. And on. And on. Lucky if we're done by three thirty. Still, it's a good chance to mock older siblings for strange and deviant choice of clothes, hair, etc.

And in between...
    Well, Mum's always on at me to go running with her in the morning, so I try to a couple of times a week. I know she misses having Hannah and Debs around. Pete? Well, he's never going to shift his bum out of bed before the absolute last minute, is he?

Violin practice. Ugh!

Domestic stuff. I do my bit. I'd do it, even if the rest of the tribe weren't so big time on my case. In my humble opinion, I do it better than they do. No bits left on the carpet after *my* session with the Dyson. Nor do I avoid grappling with the Toilet Duck, like some.

Friends. Yes, I do still have friends. All of them with umpteenth-generation mobile phones, which make tea, monitor the universe for extraterrestrial life etc etc, unlike my dinosaur model. Though, usually when they phone, they want something. Strange, that! When I phone or text, it's to see how someone is, or invite them down the cinema or Café Doppio. And in reverse? More like an advice and counselling service. Anything from help with the maths homework to definitions of date-rape.

That's it. Another week, another wad. In my case, that'll be five pounds pocket money plus expenses. All to be tightly, minutely accounted to the Family Financial Planning Manager otherwise known as My Pa.

Is it something about me? Or is everyone's life like this, whizzing round faster and faster? Stop the world, I want to get off!

And now I'm going to have a little rant.

Frankly, what really gets up my nostrils is that while everyone's so on my back to do what floats their boat, 24/7, I never see anyone else quite so flat out and frantic. Flat out maybe. Frantic, not! For instance:

I know for a fact Mum manages a little snooze most afternoons, which, at her age (44), is just gross. Fair enough, she does stuff (half a week paid in the church office, voluntary work, Board of Visitors at the local prison, that kind of thing), but Mrs McDonagh comes in twice a week to give the house a professional polish, and we eat a lot of Marks and Sparks fire-and-forget food, so she's not exactly rushed off her feet domestically, is she? What's to recover from?

And Dad? Well, let's make allowances for his advanced age (55) and the fact that I don't know what he was like when he worked for the bank. (He retired early with a nice fat pension five years ago.) For all I know he might have been Mr Go-Getter 1978. But this 'consultancy' stuff he does now doesn't seem like it interferes with his golf too much. Or the tennis club. Or the stamp collecting. Or his Sunday afternoon zizz. I could go on.

Pete would probably trot out his hormones as the reason why at

17 he's such a complete and utter lazy slob. But hey, I'm 14 next birthday (14 February – aah!), and I've got hormones of my own, right!

Airhead Hannah's living in sin with Dirty Dan her boyfriend and pretending to do Sociology at Leicester Uni. Whatever Hannah does, she always does v-e-r-y s-l-o-w-l-y. No nervous exhaustion there.

Now she's got her own flat, we don't see so much of Debs these days. Which is rancid, 'cos she is definitely My Big Sister. Debs is very calm. You always get the feeling there's loads going on in her life, but it never gets to her. I have to squeeze her to tell me anything. She just seems to take everything as it comes. I'd *like* to be like Debs, but I'm worried I'm so not. I don't think she'd waste her breath letting off steam like this, for a start. So I make an exception for Debs when I say that everyone in my family thinks they can click their fingers from the comfort of the sofa and I'll jump, any time of the day or night.

Buddies? Well, best friend Em (full name Emily Louisa Bradley)… she's really conscientious. But she doesn't do the stuff I do outside school, she doesn't lift a finger at home, and she's an atheist, she says, so no church.

Drew Chapple gets by. He'll probably surprise us all and get straight A*s for his GCSEs, if there still *are* GCSEs by then, but as far as I can see, he just coasts. Minimum action. Maximum anxiety. And congenitally incapable of making a decision about anything. Maybe that's why, like Em, Drew claims to be permanently stressed out. And in both cases I refer you to my comments above about phone manners.

Then there are the other people in my life: the teachers at what I shall have to get used to calling Willowmede *Academy*; Jana and the other dog-collars at St Michael's; Ciarán at the Dance School. It always seems to matter so much to all and sundry that 'you don't let us down, Abi'. As they sometimes so charmingly put it! But do I exist just for their benefit? I don't think so! Does their future depend on my success? For their sakes, I jolly well hope not.

Though, a lot of the time, they act like it does. Go get your own lives, guys! Who's the one really working round here?

OK, that's the rant over. There was a programme on the telly last night. One of those where there's a bunch of people high up in the Himalayas, kayaking down some bluey-green ice-melt river. For a while the river's powerful but smooth, and the canoes make their way serenely downstream. Everything's teeth and smiles. Then suddenly, whoosh, they're in the maelstrom of the rapids, the world goes mad, and suddenly one or two of the canoes are upside down with bodies hanging off them and the paddles all smashed. The music hits a grimy groove, and you don't know whether everyone's been battered to pieces on the rocks, or whether next thing they'll be found laughing and hanging on to a bush at the side of the torrent.

Well, that's me, today and tomorrow. Today = last day of the summer holidays. Tomorrow = first day of the new term. Today, total serenity. Tomorrow, madness and chaos.

So welcome to the Year Nine white water, and hang on to your hard hats. Don't rely on me to keep any kind of a diary going: I've tried it before and can't get into that every-night-before-bed thing. But Drew says blogging's the new rock'n'roll, so I'll give it a go and check in with some words at the end of every week. Then we'll see what's left of this expedition at Christmas.

Because there's always a story to any term, isn't there? I wonder what the story of this one will be?

Nothing's ever what you think, is it? The first thing I hadn't reckoned on was a total world record-breaking heatwave for the first week back at school. 9JE were three down before Monday's assembly was halfway through. Jane Pitcher keeled over first, though she'll fall in a dead faint if you whisper 'spider!' in her ear, then Melanie Appleyard, and after her Prithi Shah. The boys were killing themselves laughing, though Adam Parsons for one looked a bit green. Well, it was about 110 degrees in the school hall. The heating was full on, and the big windows were apparently stuck shut.

'I think it's me next,' Em muttered, wobbling slightly on her long legs.

'Don't you dare,' I said, doing a quick *plié* or two to keep the blood circulating. I could feel the sweat trickling down my back, and it was only nine thirty. 'We're in this together, girl.'

The next thing was the problem with the Humanities and Creative Arts Blocks. According to Big Ben (Mr Browning, our headteacher), they had something called concrete cancer.

'What did he say?' Em whispered, shuffling from foot to foot, and taking deep breaths.

'The buildings are falling down.'

'Oh!' she said, gulping for air, and looking feeble. I got ready to catch her.

The gist of the concrete thing is that for a term or two, to avoid valuable pupils being crushed by careless masonry, Years Eight and Nine will be having their Humanities and Creative Arts lessons down the road in the newly vacated premises of Brooklands Primary School. The primary school doesn't need them because they've just moved into their brand spanking new buildings close by.

11

'Fine,' hissed Em, indignation getting the better of lack of oxygen. 'Let the little kiddies have all the fun then. We'll just clean up their mess, shall we?'

Which was broadly the idea. Because since there'd been no thought that anyone was ever going to use the old Brooklands school again before it was pulled down, the place was apparently a total tip. It seemed we were going to have the privilege of making it habitable again.

The last thing was that Mr Feltham the biology teacher had pegged it during the summer break. A heart attack. He can't have been older than Dad, which is a pretty horrible thought. We had him in Year Seven and he was dead useless then. Now he's just dead. What a terrible thing to say! True though. I wonder if he's got any family? He might have kids. Don't think about it!

The next couple of days we wandered backwards and forwards carrying things into Brooklands, and suffering the occasional lesson. They let us move a few chairs around too. The teachers all looked slightly spooked in case they were breaking any health and safety rules that meant they were about to get sued rotten. What with the mind-blowing heat and the lack of organization, it was all slightly weird.

'So welcome to the new Academy,' said Drew cynically. 'Isn't it just *so* much better than the old School?'

'Lovely!' I said, dumping a pile of dog-eared copies of Shakespeare's *Julius Caesar* (the idiot's edited highlights version) onto a shelf.

During the summer, Willowmede has changed its name from being a plain boring old 'Comprehensive School' to being a supposedly much posher sounding 'Academy', which means that from now on it's going to specialize in PE. The deal is that Big Ben has got his bony hands on a shedload of new money to build sports halls and running tracks and so on. The first stage was completed during the holidays: a beautiful new state-of-the-art theatre, though what that's got to do with PE I don't know. The downside? Even before the concrete cancer scare, we'd known for ages we were going to work in something resembling a building site for the next year or so.

When the Academy idea was announced early last year, it set off all kinds of rumours. Each year group and their parents were given an evening to third-degree Mr Browning and the governors about it.

After half an hour of waffle from Big Ben explaining the architect's designs, it had to be my dad who interrupted with:

'So what I want to know is, what difference will it *actually* make to my daughter's education?'

He can sound so rude sometimes.

'Dad!' I hissed, practically crawling under the chair with embarrassment. Big Ben sat down and gave way to our Head of Year, AD, who was clearly itching to stick his greasy oar in.

'Well, Mr Goodenough,' said AD smoothly, smiling his famous trademark oily smile, 'If I could put it in two words for you, I think it might be *"Added value"*. Knowing Abi as I do – ' and here he turned a five-star smirk on me, ' – I can honestly say it will just add to the opportunities she has for using her many talents to the full…'

All around us, you could almost hear the hisses and boos rising up from the other kids and parents like poison gas. If AD's words weren't worth a beating on the way home from school one dark night sometime soon, I didn't know what was. Thank you so much!

'So it's not just going to be multigyms and squash courts for the sixth form then?'

'No, not at all,' continued AD, the grin becoming slightly more forced and fixed. 'Though obviously we'll be aiming to provide a fully enhanced sports curriculum for everyone, including Years Twelve and Thirteen. You could say we're returning to that old educational idea of *mens sana in corpore sano*…'

AD paused, and everyone looked blank. This seemed to include Big Ben.

'Perhaps you could just explain that a bit further, Dr Dickson,' he said, rather heavily. 'For those of us, like myself, who don't have any Latin…'

'I'm so sorry! *Mens sana in corpore sano* – a fit body in a fit

13

mind,' AD smarmed, clearly enjoying being one up on his boss in public. Em, who was sitting next to me, nudged me in the ribs and raised one eyebrow smirkily.

'Would you say AD's got a fit body or a fit mind?' she whispered loudly in my ear.

I giggled, audibly enough that one or two people looked round, and Dad laid a restraining hand on my knee, his turn to be embarrassed. So that was quits then!

All that was back last year. Now this week, the sun has beaten down on our hot little heads as we've repeatedly skirted the high chain link fence surrounding what used to be the school playground. We've watched as the bulldozers have pulled up the tarmac and scraped holes for the new sports hall's foundations. The air's been thick with dust. When we've actually had lessons on what's now known as the 'Main Campus', they've been interrupted by the banging of metal and the occasional machine gun burst of pneumatic drills. I've come home with a headache most days. But next year it'll be marvellous, won't it? We'll all be able to work out in the school's new multigym before the start of each day. I don't think!

In between the heatstroke, the forced labour and the industrial pollution, I couldn't avoid various teachers cornering me at unguarded moments during the week, all wanting stuff. Some were friendly. Some loomed.

First of the loomers was Miss Watkinson. Like all PE teachers, Miss Watkinson seems to think that thumbscrews or a gun in the small of the back is the only way to get a result. Do they train with the SAS or something?

'Abigail!' she shouted, from about fifty yards away. This was just as I was trying to get out of the school gates on Tuesday afternoon. Watkinson's got a voice like a sonic boom: it was no use pretending I hadn't heard. I sighed and trailed back to where she stood outside the school office.

'Swimming...' she said, without any preliminary nicety like,

'How are you? Have you had a good holiday? Isn't the weather hot?'

'... Tuesday and Thursday mornings. Six thirty. Town Baths. You'll be there, I hope? To keep us all company...' There was a mad, bad and dangerous-to-know glint in her eye.

Now this was completely out of order, because Watkinson's swimming isn't even really a school activity. It's more like a bit of private enterprise. She's a big cheese in the County Swimming Association, and true, once a year they run a gala for schools, but so what? And like, *six thirty*? In the *morning*? Let's get real here!

'Probably not, Miss Watkinson,' I said, facing her down while smiling sweetly. With PE teachers it seems to me the principles are the same as training a dog with bad habits and a nasty bite. I pretended to be giving the matter due consideration. Then I did some more acting and added uncertainly, 'It's difficult...'

'Disappointing,' she growled. 'Success isn't always about natural talent, you know. Hard yards, Abigail, hard yards. I thought you'd understand that!'

'I'm sorry,' I said, making like I really was, and backing away slowly. I could see that if I wasn't careful, she was going to go into her speech about being prepared to break through the pain barrier. (For the record I'm not. Not as far as swimming goes, anyway!)

'Mum's waiting for me... The mornings at home... They're complicated, you know. Sorry, Miss Watkinson. Maybe next year...?'

As I went, I thought, *Now she'll start thinking I have to look after baby brothers or sisters or something. Or that I've got a disabled parent. She'll probably check up. I bet I haven't heard the last of that one.*

On the other hand, Sandy Johnson, the drama teacher, was really nice when he sidled up to me at break on Wednesday morning.

'How's about I make you a star?' he said softly, and I jumped, not having heard him coming. Mr Johnson looks rather like a movie star himself. Perhaps slightly too much so. A bit careful with it? Think two parts Pierce Brosnan and one part Ewan McGregor. Handsome in a sort of old and creased kind of way.

'Pardon?'

'I know I'm a fool to myself,' he said, 'but I'm going to try another school production, now I've recovered from my last nervous breakdown. *The Crucible*. Ever heard of it?'

I hadn't.

'Well, it's a simply marvellous piece of drama, Abi. Everyone should do *The Crucible* once in their life. It's about persecution, and why people jump on bandwagons. Really important stuff. And funnily enough, one of the characters is called Abigail. So I thought of you. Interested?'

I said I might be.

'Fantastic! Auditions early next term. Showtime at Easter. It'd be great to have you on board. OK?'

And Mr Johnson smiled in that confidential, you-are-the-only-person-who-matters-in-the-whole-world manner he has. Which doesn't fool me for one moment. Might still do the play though.

By Wednesday afternoon, the classrooms at Brooklands were more or less finally sorted, and not their former squalid selves. So hey-ho, there was no avoiding top set French with Mr Farthing, known to everyone as 'Penny' for obvious reasons.

Penny is one of those teachers who always beams at people he's taken a shine to, of whom unfortunately I am one (despite all my best efforts to persuade him otherwise), and scowls at everyone else. It doesn't do a lot for peer-group relationships in the classroom, if you get me.

I do not like French or Mr Penny. I mean, Mr Farthing. There really is a severe danger I'll call him by the wrong name one day.

I was sneaking out after the lesson, and thought I'd made it safely, when I heard him call after me. I turned back. Penny's style is the iron threat in the velvet voice. He often wears a suede jacket, which tells you a lot, I think.

'Just a word,' he murmured. 'I wondered, have you thought about your GCSE options yet?'

I shook my head. 'Not really,' I said weakly.

'We'd be happy to have you in the German set, Abigail,' he said silkily. 'You could easily make a success of foreign languages at A

16

level.'

What was the man talking about? Here I am, just starting Year Nine, and already he's wanting me to sign up to what I'll be doing in three years' time. Now, I'm not stupid: I can see what Penny's after. No A level students means no power, and no way am I going to be part of his empire-building. Without committing myself, I tried to say that all things were possible, and mentally kept my fingers crossed. Only mentally mind, because my hands were occupied holding onto my bag and a pile of books.

Then, would you believe it, on Thursday morning Miss Everard – her of the County Youth Choir – started off on the same tack, only this time for Music GCSE. Except in her socially challenged case, instead of wheedling, she had me sort of backed against a wall in a corridor. Everard is one of those people who always comes too close to you, right up in your face, so that to avoid their bad breath you find yourself having conversations on the walk. On a bad day you can cover hundreds of metres going backwards while she tells you stuff you don't want to know like what to wear for a concert or whether Mozart died in poverty. But this time I had nowhere to hide.

'If good students like you don't opt for music, the course won't run,' she started aggressively.

Your problem, lady. If you were a better teacher more kids would want to do your subject.

'... And with your ability there'd be a guaranteed A, maybe even an A* if you put in the work...'

And with your ability, you'll probably teach us the wrong syllabus and everyone will fail...

'And if you're thinking about music as a career, you really need this under your belt...'

But I'm not, am I? How many times do I have to tell you...

And so on and so on. I hummed and ha-ed, and eventually she went away, thinking she was still in with a chance. Maybe I should have put her out of her misery, and told her straight, 'Everard, while you're in charge, there's no way in a million years I'd ever do Music,' but she probably wouldn't have taken any notice even then.

What we school students need are agents, like footballers have. Then, before signing up for a subject, we could negotiate the deal: the best seats in class, an end to sarcasm, the guaranteed return of work on time, more mufti days, that sort of thing. Of course, a transfer fee would be nice too…

Then finally, at Friday lunchtime in the hall, while I was innocently munching my salad, enjoying my own company for a few seconds, and hiding from the heat and dust, AD suddenly materialized in front of me. *Doctor* Adrian Dickson. Head of Year Nine. Our great leader. Respect, respect.

He's not a medical doctor, of course. It just means he's done even more exams than everyone else. And he *is* obviously very brainy. You can just tell. There's a sort of force field around his head. He's hyperactive too. If he was a kid, they'd be feeding him ritalin to slow him down, like they did with James Phillips in primary school. Which is maybe how he does that materializing thing. I mean, if there's a fight between two of the boys, I guarantee you AD will be there within ten seconds of anything starting.

He hovered above the lunch table for a moment, and then said, almost furtively, 'Can I join you?'

Which was nice of him to ask. Most teachers wouldn't.

I swallowed a mouthful of rabbit food, and said, yes, sure, no problem. He sat down.

'Thing is, Abi, there's something I want to put to you. Have you got a minute?'

I nodded, but the little grey matter was whizzing a bit. Had Penny or Everard complained? Or was he going to go off on one too, and tell me I should be a brain surgeon, and do science all day every day for the next ten years? Then I had the dizzying thought that something had happened to Mum or Dad, and he'd come to break the bad news. But no, I needn't have worried.

'I've been a bit concerned…' he said, his brow furrowing. '… Actually, more than a bit concerned. I think we've been letting our brighter people – like you – well, I think we've not been doing the best we can for you?'

He said it with an upturn in his voice at the end of the sentence, like the characters do with every sentence in *Neighbours*. It suits people my age with micro-skirts and Britney hair, but it sounds forced coming from him. Sometimes AD's voice even *sounds* a bit Australian.

He looked genuinely anxious. I nodded encouragingly. He was trying to be nice, even if I knew that, like everyone else, in the end he probably wanted something, like more of my precious time.

'So Abi, during the summer, I've been doing some thinking and planning, and what I've come up with is this. I want to start an "Achievers' Club" for Willowmede's Year Nine…?'

There was the *Neighbours* thing again.

'… A series of events to get your brains really moving, and give you the extra you deserve. And Abi, you're one of the first people I thought of. What do you say?'

'Sounds great,' I found myself saying, as if at that moment an alien had taken over my brain. 'Cool!' While all the time my proper self was thinking, *Teacher-pleasing plonker! Just say that one little word. Say no! Now. Do it. How hard can that be?*

'Well, now I know you're interested,' he said, looking really perky, 'I just need to get round a few more people. Like maybe Charlotte Ellison?'

He was studying me to see the reaction he was getting. I don't mind Char Ellison: she's loud and a bit posh but she can be quite funny when she tries.

'And of the boys, perhaps Drew Chapple and Eddie Finn…'

That struck a slightly odd note. Of course, Drew's a mate, so that was perfectly OK, but from what I'd heard about Eddie (he's in 9SP so I haven't actually seen that much of him), the boy's a bit of a weirdo. Still, weird can be interesting, so why not?

'Emily Bradley would probably be up for it too,' I suggested. Now it was AD's turn to be caught off guard. Obviously Em hadn't been on his shortlist, which personally I thought was a bit steep. It's not like she's the new Carol Vorderman, but she's not exactly thick either.

'Yeah, that'd be great,' AD replied, a bit too quickly, his eyes a bit glazed and not quite in sync with his mouth (what has Em done to upset AD?). 'Anyway, I thought if we all got together next Wednesday lunchtime, I could fill you in with some of the things I had in mind. Is that OK?'

'Fine,' I said. 'No worries!' The alien was in complete control. Ga-ga-oo-gooh-doo-wop-tharg!

Next time just say no, Abi! It's so simple! You really don't need any more things to do!

Blog the Second
18 September

'What's all this stuff about your new club, Abs?'

That was Char Ellison on Tuesday morning, talking to the whole of south Leicestershire in her usual foghorn voice, while I tried to coax my locker shut using both violence and persuasion. They could use Char to do the announcements on Sports Day and forget the public address system.

'Bit keen isn't it?' she added.

'What new club?' I said, not putting two and two together. Then the penny dropped.

'Oh! *That!* Look, it's not *my* new club. AD's a total ratfink. It's all his big idea. I just said I might go along...'

Char shrugged. 'Well, whatever, it sounded quite good to me,' she said. 'I thought, well done Abi. After all, this place needs a bit of livening up. Sometimes I'm so bored I think I'll stand up in class and say the rudest thing I know just to see what happens.'

'You know what happens,' I said. 'They'd exclude you for two days, then you'd say sorry and promise not to do it again, and then you'd do it again, and then they'd exclude you for a few days and then...'

'So you *are* going tomorrow? To this meeting?'

I said I supposed so, even if AD was a toad.

'Good,' said Char. 'Can't wait to meet Sam Saward!'

'Who's Sam Saward?' I asked.

Of course, as soon as I'd asked the question I remembered. Sam Saward had been the manager of England's World Cup winning rugby team. Even I knew that. Char's notorious for being a mad keen rugby player, so AD's mention of his name was always going to light up her radar, and he probably knew it. Is it the game or the boys with Char? I've never been sure. Though she is built for it.

Rugby, that is.

'Anyway, what's Sam Saward got to do with anything?'

'Old friend of AD's apparently. They were at uni together.'

Well that figured, but it still didn't fully answer my question.

'So he's going to be here tomorrow then, is he?'

'No. AD's got him lined up for some talk thing later in the term.'

Wednesday lunchtime there we were in the Meeting Room, which is actually the nicest place in school, just off the library. It's very strange, but when I'm in there I feel sort of cleaner, more organized and altogether more like a proper person than I do anywhere else in Willowmede. The chairs are comfortable, there's a nice long rectangular table, and on the tops of the bookshelves there are some lovely bits of sculpture left behind by long-gone star A level students. This is going to make me sound 80 years old or something, but the Meeting Room really is quite civilized. Char was there, and Em, and Drew, looking freckle-faced after the week of sun. (The weather's gone normal on us by the way. Wind and rain followed by rain and wind. So now we get grit blown in our eyes every time we scuttle between lessons!)

Eddie Finn sat on his own, sallow-skinned, slightly rat-like, fiddling with his dirty nails, his eyes hidden by a mop of greasy long black hair. Eddie doesn't appear to look at anyone, unless he thinks they're not looking at him. There were a couple of other kids too. I didn't know either of them at all because they're in the other half-year. There was Sally something-I-didn't-catch with a very Scottish accent, and a smartly dressed kid called Sylvester Young, who looked eager to please and alarmed by turns. AD had brought along Miss Hughes, his sidekick. I think she's a Zoe. She teaches science – the same as AD – and she's always seemed nice enough, the little I've seen of her, covering the odd lesson when teachers have been off sick. She *is* very pretty, which is exactly what you'd expect of a female henchperson to AD.

AD did a 'Thank you all for coming' thing, and launched into his spiel about the 'Achievers' Club'. A few features gradually began to emerge from the fog.

'I thought we'd organize some weekend trips...' he began.

You've got to admire AD in a way. He'd make an excellent salesman – far better than those morons who ring up at seven thirty on a Monday evening when you're all settling down to Corrie and chips, and mumble hopelessly about double glazing. So how did he end up in teaching? Must be more money in it, I suppose. Anyway, this was him softening us up with a few bribes.

'... The Leicester Haymarket Theatre have said they're happy to give us a tour backstage with a chance to meet the *Jailhouse Rock* touring company...'

That sounded good to me, though Drew made like he was having his teeth pulled. As far as Drew's concerned, culture means the Saturday night lottery show on TV.

'... And, though we'd need a whole Saturday, I'd like us to visit the Tate Modern gallery in London?'

Now that was cool. London. And the gallery. Drew looked ever so slightly more interested in this, but probably only because he'd heard about the Tate's 'Nudes Make News' exhibition which opened this week. On Monday one of the tabloid newspapers had run a headline which said, 'Stark Staring Bonkers'. Look, don't blame me, blame big brother Pete! He buys the silly, stupid comics and leaves them lying around, just to annoy Mum. It works, every time!

'... Apart from Sam Saward's keynote talk in a fortnight's time, which you'll see is called 'How to Win Big!', we've some other really exciting speakers lined up for occasional workshops and sessions. Haven't we, Miss Hughes?'

Zoe Hughes had brought a lunchtime cup of coffee with her, and was taking frequent sips. AD's question caught her mid-gulp, the coffee went down the wrong way, and she spluttered and tried to nod her head at the same time. Unkindly, we all laughed. To be fair, she joined in, once she'd stopped choking.

'Could we have a famous pop singer or actor?' interrupted Em. 'Like Keira Knightley. Or Girls On Motorbikes?'

Duh! Bang went my attempts to give Em a bit of cred in AD's

eyes. He gave her a pitying stare, before remembering he was trying to be Mr Motivator here.

'Thanks for that, Emily. Maybe we could arrange something of the sort for next term. Of course, if you know anyone who'd like to visit Willowmede, then that would be great. But remember these kinds of people have very full diaries...'

That was a 'no' then, was it?

'Can *anyone* come to these meetings?' Sylvester asked, which was an intelligent question. I'd been wondering the same thing myself.

'Yes, absolutely!' beamed AD. 'And if you look on the school calendar, you'll see all the evening meetings are posted there.'

I hadn't looked at my school calendar, which had only been handed out during the morning, so I didn't know that.

'Letters will go out tomorrow to all Willowmede families about the Sam Saward reception, and since the local Chamber of Commerce is sponsoring the evening, we're anticipating a lot of outside visitors. In fact, we'd like your help with the stewarding, if that's OK?'

Funnily enough that was very OK as far as I was concerned. I really like all that showing people to their seats and 'would you like a cup of coffee' stuff. Can't you just imagine me at home, going 'Dad, I've decided. I want to be an usherette'?

AD was unstoppable now.

'... Although I'd imagined some of the sessions, like the meditation workshop Jana Zhivanovic is leading in November, might be rather more just for us. But I don't think there should be anything exclusive here. We don't want to keep anyone out!'

Jana had kept the meditation thing quiet. She's the youth leader at St Michael's, my church, and a favourite person, most of the time. Very calm, very good to talk to in a crisis.

'Talking of the Chamber of Commerce,' AD continued, 'we'd like you to take part in their "Junior Business of the Year" competition next July...'

He must have caught the wave of apathy wafting back at him from around the table, because he promptly pulled back from that one.

'... Of course, we wouldn't need to think about that until the New Year. And I suppose there'd be no point in entering at all, unless we'd come up with an absolutely stonking business plan...'

Stonking. The kind of word adults like AD use to show how up to date and trendy they are. Oh dear! Go back four spaces and down the snake of cool, Adrian.

After that the only other headline seemed to be stuff about putting something back into the community. Shopping for old dears, I suppose, or something similar.

Everyone chipped in with a question or two except Char and Sally. Odd thing. Char had looked miserable right through the meeting, as if she'd rather have been anywhere else. There hadn't even been a flicker at the mention of her hero, Sam Saward. I'd tried to catch her eye once or twice, but she hadn't wanted to know. That girl's moods swing like a yo-yo.

Then, when AD seemed to be finally running out of steam, Sally What's-her-name suddenly piped up in one of his pauses for breath. Her voice was thin and clear and precise.

'So what's in it for us then?' she said. Narrowed, piercing eyes. Not the hint of a smile.

It was a very direct question, right up there with my dad in the rudeness stakes. For a moment you could hear nothing but the quiet tick of the Meeting Room clock. Everyone was suddenly riveted.

But surprisingly, instead of being mightily hacked off, AD's face creased into an amused grin. 'Quite right!' he said, a bit wolfishly. 'Absolutely right. This might all sound like we just want to do more stuff to you. But honestly, that wasn't the idea. We want to make school better. Give you more energy. We know that if you're bright and have ambition, it can sometimes be hard to see above the daily grind. Isn't that right, Miss Hughes?'

Hughesey nodded vigorously. She'd finished her coffee so she could give the nod full welly without fear of imminent death by choking.

'We don't want you to feel we always trundle along at the pace of the slowest. And if the "Achievers' Club" isn't a bit of fun as well as a bit of challenge, well then, it won't be worth doing.'

He was good, I'll give him that. Sally looked like she was convinced. And I know I felt a bit of a lift, that *they* thought *we* were worth the effort. Maybe it was the aliens at work again.

But the non-alien voice inside my head, the cynical old Abi, was saying, *Yeah, but it won't do you any harm either will it, AD, if this is all a raging success? Because we're not the only ones with ambition here, are we?*

Was that very unfair of me?

As soon as AD wound things up, Char grabbed her bag and made smartly for the door like there was a train to catch. No goodbye. A suspicion of dampness around the eyes. Em and I swapped glances, and I went in pursuit. Well, you've got to look out for each other, haven't you? I caught Char up halfway to the school gates.

'You OK?' I said.

She had her head down into the wind, hunched down in her anorak. She didn't look up.

'Yeah, yeah, fine,' she muttered.

'Anything I can do?'

'No. No! I told you. I'm fine.'

'OK,' I said, running to keep up. 'Look, you know you can talk to me. Any time. Right?'

'Yeah, I know that,' she said, slightly less savagely. 'Thanks, Abi. You're all right. It's just… It's just… Oh, I expect it'll go away!'

'OK!'

I gave up the chase, and she was gone. Presumably whatever was eating at her was nothing to do with the 'Achievers' Club'. But what, then?

Incidentally, I'm not sure my coolness rating allows me to belong to something called the 'Achievers' Club'! Definitely *nul points* for style. I think the same kind of thing had been in Eddie's mind when he'd politely interrupted AD's speech back in the Meeting Room.

'Excuse me, Dr Dickson,' he'd said, peering up from inside the curtain of hair which fell greasily across his forehead. Eddie speaks in a strange, nasal tone of voice, like there's something permanently stuck up his nose. He was surprisingly polite and tactful though.

'It's the name,' he droned, adenoidally. 'I mean, I'm sure it's a good name, and like, it does what it says on the tin. But don't you think kids will think it's just for nerds? They might even, you know, want to give us a bagging just for belonging.'

The nasal impediment made this last sentence particularly amusing to someone like me with a warped sense of humour. Try pinching your nose with a thumb and forefinger and say 'bagging' to get the Finn effect. AD looked serious. Maybe, like us, he was sizing Eddie up at that moment, and thinking, *Is this kid bully fodder or what?*. Whatever, it seemed like he got Eddie's point.

'Well…' he said, buying himself thinking time, and looking across at Zoe Hughes, who was in turn looking out of the window. Perhaps she'd already decided it was a naff moniker, and it was a case of 'Told you so!'.

'The notices in the calendar just say what's happening on the various evenings. Nowhere have we yet mentioned the "Achievers' Club" explicitly. So, if you've any suggestions, let's meet same time same place next week, and come armed with your alternative names. Is that OK, Eddie?'

As far as anyone could tell, Eddie the tortoise looked satisfied as he withdrew into his shell of hair.

Talking about Eddie, Em and I ran into him unexpectedly, late on Saturday afternoon. One of the things us two girls like to do every now and then is catch a bus into town and go to the cinema. It's funny how the two of us are such complete physical opposites but still get on like a house on fire. Maybe it's *because* we're so different. If Em's a giraffe, then I suppose I'm a koala, though maybe that's a bit unfair to both of us. What I'm trying to say is, she's got long beanpole legs and has to stoop to talk to me, because I'm short and compact. Her nose is long and angular; mine's slightly squashed and stubby. She has shoulder-length wispy blonde hair that straggles round her face; mine is dark and wiry, and would be like a bush if I let it grow it too long. And so on and so on.

Anyway, usually we go down to the flicks a bit early, sit in Café Doppio and gossip before the film starts. Then we get a doting parent, usually Em's, to come and collect us afterwards. This time the stupid bus broke down two or three stops before town, and rather than sit there and wait for a replacement, we decided life was too short and hoofed it by the shortest route, cutting off a corner by the university. There was a fine, chilling drizzle in the air, but it wasn't actually pouring with rain like it's done all day today.

Suddenly, there in front of us was a small, hunched, rat-like figure, unmistakably our Eddie, trailing forlornly down the road in his too-large army surplus parka, looking like a refugee. He was walking very slowly, about half the speed we were, so it wasn't long before we were almost level with him.

It was one of those situations where you don't quite know how to handle saying hello to someone. Em completely blew it because when she said in her normal friendly voice, 'Hey Eddie!' from about two feet behind Eddie's right ear, he jumped like he'd been stung by a swarm of wasps.

Now we were parallel with him, we could see he looked frozen stiff. And guilty, like we'd caught him out somehow. I tried to jolly things along by saying something like, 'What's going down, Eddie?', but he went all peculiar on us.

'Nothing. Wasn't doing nothing,' he twitched.

'OK! No worries!' I said, wrong-footed by the twitching. 'You going into town, then?'

'Nah. Not particularly...' He really was shaking, backing away from us like a puppy that's been mistreated, his face obscured inside the helmet of his hair, hands thrust deep inside his parka's pockets.

'Right,' Em added limply, as we sort of slowly circled Eddie, feeling vaguely responsible. 'Well then, have a nice day, Ed. See ya!' And on we walked to the city centre and the six o'clock showing of the new Jake Gyllenhaal.

'What was all that about?' Em went when we were out of earshot. 'Did he look guilty or what?'

'Yeah, but why?'

'Search me!'

'I felt sorry for him, didn't you? I mean, like we should have invited him to come down the flicks with us…'

Em made a 'you've gotta be joking' face.

'… Yeah, OK! Really bad idea. Someone might see us!'

'Well, what's he up to? Eddie doesn't live round here, does he?' asked Em.

'Shouldn't think so, would you?' I said, waving a hand at the posh houses behind the railings we were passing. 'Bit out of Eddie's league, I reckon.'

'Ours too,' said Em wistfully. 'Wouldn't it be great to have electronic gates and fountains and stuff?'

'Well, you'll just have to win the lottery, won't you!'

Since yesterday afternoon I've just not been able to get that picture of guilty little Eddie Finn out of my head. What with his air of mystery, Sally's courtroom manner and Char's mood swings we're certainly running with some weird dudes in this *Future Rulers of the World Club*, or whatever it's going to be called!

Em breezed into Willowmede on Monday morning, full of energy, bouncing off things and people like they weren't there. (There you are again – she's an early morning person. I improve the longer the day goes on.)

'Got it,' she football-chanted across the desks at me. 'I've got it!'

'Well, whatever it is,' I shouted back, 'keep it to yourself. *I* don't want it. You've been at the zinc and vitamin C bottle again, haven't you? How many times have I got to tell you. If you're not careful, they'll be sending round those nice men in white coats.'

Actually, me, I was feeling fairly rancid, what with a dull headache and the beginnings of what was probably the September back-to-school cold. Probably not *enough* zinc and vitamin C.

'It's dead simple,' she said.

'What?'

'It's got to be the A Club.'

'Come again?'

'The A Club! The *Achievers' Club*, dummy!'

The thing is that really, despite AD's prejudice, Em's the one who's keenest on this whole caper. So whereas I hadn't given a moment's thought to the matter of the name all weekend, clearly it had been whirring round and round in what Em laughingly refers to as her brain.

'Lowers the tone a bit, doesn't it?' I said.

'Well, wasn't that what Eddie was on about?'

'Yeah, but… 'A' Club… 'S' Club…Think about it, Em! Do you really want to remind people of pop posters you had on your bedroom wall in Year Four?'

Em hadn't thought of that. She looked sceptical.

'It wouldn't do that. Would it?'

I made a face suggesting it probably would.

'Oh,' she said, clearly a bit deflated, 'I thought it was kind of cool and anonymous, and wouldn't have people asking questions. The A said "achievement" without actually saying it, if you see what I mean.'

I *did* see. I didn't like to see Em looking crushed.

'No, look, it's a good idea,' I said. 'And far better than any I've had, because I haven't had any. So let's see whether anything else comes up before Wednesday. If it doesn't, well personally, the A Club gets my vote!'

Funnily enough, as morning became afternoon, the name began to grow on me. I even started to think it *would* be cool to remind people of their infant days with S Club. Isn't that what they call ironic?

At break on Monday, Char came and found me. When I'd seen her around Willowmede on Thursday, she'd still seemed fed up and unapproachable. On Friday she'd simply not been in school. Today she seemed quiet, but OK.

'Would you like to come to tea tomorrow?' she said meekly.

I was touched. It was strangely old-fashioned and... nice, like we were back in one of those Miss Marple films you see on the telly.

'Yes,' I said. 'I'd love to. How do we do this, then?'

I was nosy. I knew Char's family had money, and lived in the country out towards Northampton with ponies and stuff. All rather different from us townie Goodenoughs. I wanted to know how many bedrooms and stable blocks they'd got!

'No prob!' she said. 'We'll take you and bring you back. It's cool with Mum.'

So I texted home, to make sure they were equally cool about me being away half the evening, and made a mental note to square Watkinson about missing after-school basketball just the one time. Don't want to spoil my chances of being captain, do I?

When Char's one-to-one, you can hear how posh her accent really is. When she's being loud, life-and-soul-of-the-party Char at school, she puts on a bit of street, so you don't notice the poshness.

Clever, that! And only sensible self-defence at Willowmede; the thing you have to do, to avoid being – what was it Eddie had said? – given a bagging! Though I'd like to see anyone try bagging Char! They'd probably get bagged themselves.

We *nearly* had a really good time, at least for the first three-quarters of it. Char's completely different out of school. Much more thoughtful, much more considerate. When she'd said 'come to tea', it had never crossed my mind that she'd have personally done the baking. But she had. Scones with jam and cream, and a Victoria sponge. I forgot my anti-spot rules and indulged. Very good they were too. Rugby and cooking: how does that work, then?

Char and her mum had driven me in some big Jeep thing out to where they live, which is called Thornton Bramleigh. There are high creamy white and brown stone walls all around the village between sandstone houses. There's a village green too, and a cosy-looking thatched pub. The Ellison's house isn't so amazing when it comes down to it, with four bedrooms – like ours – but there's a paddock at the back, and she *does* have a pony called Rarebit, which I thought was a clever name. Not that I'm remotely a horsey person. Can't stand the smell. Ugh!

The single thing which amazed me more than anything else was the number of books in their house. OK, we Goodenoughs have books too, but not like this. There were shelves and shelves of them: new ones, old ones, coffee-table books I half-remembered seeing in Waterstones, novels, TV books, maps, encyclopedias. You name it, they'd got it. And Char's room was much the same as the family lounge and study. Books everywhere. Piles of them on the floor. If you'd asked me beforehand, I'd have said Char was all parties and rubbing down Rarebits, but it seems what she does with her spare time is read. And read. No brothers and sisters to interrupt. No telly either, not that I saw. Which figures come to think of it, because I've never heard her join in the *EastEnders* gossip.

But wow, does she know stuff about people. It's like she's hoovering up information. After an hour with Char, I began to think

I was walking around with my eyes shut all the time.

For a start there was the skinny on Sally (whose second name is apparently Kennedy).

'Of course, her dad's a pop star,' Char said, like everyone knew that. I didn't.

'He is?'

'They're called *Wasted*, or something?'

I put two and two together.

'Her dad's *Bobby* Kennedy?'

Bobby Kennedy's the lead singer with the aforementioned *Wasted*. All I know is what I read in Pete's *Sun*. They have a certain... notoriety! The usual drugs and stuff. And Drew has one of their CDs, because he's into older stuff. The sound's loud and scuzzy, definitely music for boys. But I'm certain sure positive Drew has no idea there's a connection to Willowmede. He'd go mental with excitement. If you'd asked me, from what I'd seen over Pete's shoulder, I'd have assumed Bobby Kennedy was no more than, say, 21? Which now seemed rather unlikely.

Char seemed to have the low-down on the Willowmede teachers too.

'Of course, you know about AD and Hughesey?' she asked. I didn't.

'She used to go out with Mr Alsop till last Easter,' Char said nonchalantly. 'But now she's living with AD.'

'And you know this how?' I asked, suspiciously.

'They live in Thornton Bramleigh. Last cottage on the way out of the village. The one with the gnomes in the front garden.'

Gnomes? That had to be worth storing up for a rainy day.

And then it suddenly crossed my mind that Char was remarkably good at asking questions. She'd been doing it to me, all through tea and scones, and she was so good at it, I hadn't even really noticed. But I bet that by now there was a nice little profile marked Abi Goodenough lodged somewhere in her filing cabinet of a brain – siblings, church, dance, likes and dislikes.

'Of course, Eddie Finn's a genius with computers,' she said. 'But you knew that.'

I didn't, but I could have guessed. It's a cliché, the geek whose brain is apparently hard-wired to his PC, but Eddie fits it to a T, when you think about it. I'd wondered what the angle was on his A Club membership. Presumably this was it.

'In fact, anything practical,' said Char. 'I reckon Eddie could make a spaceship out of a ball of string and a few tin cans.' She said this so admiringly, that I double took for a moment. Char's at least twice Eddie's size and looks like she washes on a more or less daily basis, so on the face of it romantic attachment seemed a remote likelihood.

'What do you know about Sylvester then?' I asked. Char shrugged. Ha! I'd caught her out!

'Not a lot, really. His family originally came from Jamaica, but Syl was born here. He's been back there twice, but didn't like it much. He wants to be a long jumper, but he's worried his legs aren't growing fast enough. Apparently he's got an IQ above 150, and I know for a fact if you ask him he can tell you which day of the week any date in fifty or a hundred years' time will be. Oh, and he had a baby sister with a hole in the heart. They tried to do something about it, but it didn't work out and she died last year.'

So nothing in the file, really! But wow, that stuff about his sister! Poor Sylvester.

Up there in Char's room, sitting on the floor among the books, with Dido (yuk!) playing quietly on the stereo, I thought I'd turn the tables on her.

'What do your parents do, then?' I asked, still wondering where the nice house and garden, the Jeep and the horse, all came from. It didn't seem like Mrs Ellison had any sort of a job.

'Dad's got his own company,' Char said, twirling an end of thick, glossy hair between her fingers. 'Advertising and stuff. He works insanely hard. Never here.'

There was something *'ouch'* about the way she said that. It wasn't a tone of voice I'd ever use about my dad, for all that he can be a complete donkey.

And then out of the blue Char crumpled, dropping her face into her drawn-up knees and rocking gently backwards and forwards. Crying, but not making any noise with it. I was gobsmacked. Where had that come from? I waited for a moment, then shifted on my bum and sat beside her. I put an arm round her shoulders, and we just stayed like that for maybe ten minutes. I couldn't think what else to do.

Eventually, Char raised her head from the folds of her school skirt, wiped a hand across her eyes, and started to talk about herself and her parents. And once she'd begun, it was like she couldn't stop, as if she'd been saving it up for months.

Apparently whenever her parents were at home together, which wasn't often, the two of them would row. They shouted a lot at each other, and said dreadful things, and sometimes it went on so long and so late, Char was sure the neighbours could hear. Once or twice, but not when she'd been in the room, she'd heard things being thrown. Char spent as much time as she could reading because it was the only safe place she could escape to. She was lonely and frightened, because all she could think was that either the family would break up and they'd have to move from lovely Thornton Bramleigh, or that eventually her mum or her dad would hurt each other. Like *physically* hurt each other.

I was horrified. I mean, you hear about stuff like this in the papers or in books, but I've never had to deal with it in real life. I've got to say, it shook me up, rocked my world a bit.

I looked surreptitiously at my watch. I knew Mrs Ellison was expecting to take me home at seven thirty, and it was now quarter past seven.

But Char hadn't finished. Just when I thought she'd said everything there was to say, up she started again, sobbing that in the last week or two her mum had suddenly changed, that where in the past at least she'd always made the effort with Char, now she

35

was distant and cold, and her mind always seemed to be somewhere else. Once, when they'd started arguing, her mum had actually lashed out at her to try to slap her face. She'd missed, but neither of Char's parents had ever hit her, not even when she was small. So now, Char felt like she was slowly losing both parents. They were drifting away from her on the tide.

I must say, at first sight I hadn't liked Mrs Ellison. She's very tall and elegant, with fine, angular features. But she's cold too, and I got the impression her heart's as starchy as her hair. I suppose she might have been very beautiful when she was younger. She's certainly kept her figure. It sounds unkind, but Char must get her squared-off looks from her dad.

Eventually I had to say gently, 'Look Char, I'm going to have to go, aren't I? Are you going to be OK?'

She nodded tearfully, and balled up a hanky, pressing it to her eyes.

'I said, and I meant it, if you *ever* need to talk, I can be there,' I promised her. 'And if it ever came to it, there'd even be a spare bed at our house. I know Mum wouldn't mind.'

Charlotte put her arms around me and hugged me.

The journey home was monosyllabic. Maybe Mrs Ellison thought Char and I'd fallen out. She drove fast, like she wanted to get shot of me as quickly as possible. If she guessed what had really been going down, she didn't let on. Superior, nose-in-the-air, ice-queen stuff all the way.

When I closed the Goodenough front door behind me, I suddenly realized I was completely shattered, and my throat was burning. I'd been right about getting that cold. Well, on top of everything else she had to contend with, now Char was probably going to catch it too.

'There's a couple of answerphone messages for you, Abs,' Pete yelled at my back as I dragged my sorry self upstairs for a comforting bath.

Aaaargh! Wouldn't it be great to live where everyone else didn't know your business. I don't get *my* kicks listening to messages from Pete's smelly friends.

'*Message one*,' the smug female answerphone voice intoned in my ear when I'd come down half an hour later in my dressing gown for a nightcap of hot chocolate and two aspirins.

'Hi Abi! It's Jana! How's life treating you? Sorry to miss you! Wondered if you could do some prayers at St Michael's on Sunday morning? Can you ring me if you can't? Well, no, ring me anyway, and I'll tell you about it. Ciao!'

'*Message two*.'

'What? Hey! OK, yeah…'

That was Drew, confused at which was answer machine and which was real live Goodenough.

'Look Abi, I don't get the Geography homework – the map thing about Alloa? What do I do? Hey, like, call me. OK…?'

I didn't know there *was* any Geography homework. Come to that I didn't know where or what Alloa was. Somewhere near Hawaii by the sound of it, and all I know about that is flowered shirts. Drew's getting worse, I swear. Too late to phone him back, anyway, so if it was Hawaii, paradise was going to have to go on hold.

'*Message three*.' (And this message was delivered so loudly it was crackling and distorting…)

'Abigail? Are you there? It's Ciarán Barron from the Dance School. We need to talk about the Dance Festival at half-term. Can you get back to me as soon as you can, please? As soon as you can, OK? It's very important. Thank you. Don't forget!'

This term's honeymoon period was well and truly over.

I was feeling completely disgusting on Wednesday morning, sneezing every ten seconds, and producing truckloads of horrible gooey phlegm. Fed up with everyone too, and biting their heads off. A blowback from the previous evening, I suppose. But true to form, no malingering allowed in the Goodenough household, at least not for the youngest and busiest member, even if she's got flu, so I was packed off to school anyway, to spread my germs more efficiently among the population. I do not understand the sense of this attitude. And if ever I have children, I swear I will take a quite different point of view. Or at least make them wear masks.

I more or less slept through the lunchtime meeting with AD, but I guess it didn't matter because I was so obviously ill. Em's 'A Club' idea for the name was greeted with wild enthusiasm on all sides. She looked like the cat who'd just got the cream, while AD smiled indulgently on her. I spent most of the time slumped there looking stupidly at him and Hughesey, and thinking obsessively to myself, *So are they actually going home at the end of the day and* doing *it?* Nightmare stuff. Almost as bad as thinking about my parents having sex. I mean, you know it's happened (in my case, at least four times!), but it still seems completely incredible and distasteful. I wish Char hadn't told me.

Talking of Char, she was reasonably normal, just a bit subdued. Charlotte-lite, you could say. No one else would have thought anything of it.

I didn't have the energy to phone Ciarán that evening, or on the Thursday, when she tried to leave a very snotty message, which thankfully Mum intercepted after I'd already gone to bed. For once Mum put her foot down, and said Ciarán had to make allowances. Everyone got ill at some time or another, didn't they? So she should just back off. Hallelujah! Parents do occasionally have their uses.

But on Friday, my conscience got the better of me and even though I was still feeling like a drugged zombie, I called in to see Ciarán at the Dance School on the way home from Willowmede.

The dingy brown corridor leading to the changing room smelt badly of sweaty bodies, like always. The paint on the walls and ceiling gave in to the sweat long ago, and only about half of it is left. In studio 1, Ciarán was putting the junior jazz class through a pumpingly vigorous routine. Or it would have been if they could have told their right feet from their left.

'Ah, Abigail!' she shouted across the studio above the deafening sound of 'The Hustle'. 'At last! 1, 2, 3, 4, 5, 6, 7, 8… Turn! And run! Go on! I mean really running! Not taking a Sunday afternoon stroll!'

Ciarán's got a voice like a chainsaw: it cuts through any amount of noise around it. Mum says Ciarán was starting to teach when Mum and Dad got married, so that's twenty-three years of shouting like a fishwife, eight hours a day, six days a week. It's a wonder she hasn't got nodules on her vocal chords, like pop singers get.

'Maddie dear, you take over, while I talk to Abigail,' she bawled at sidekick Madeleine Grimshaw. Madeleine is 18, wants to be a professional dancer, and in my humble opinion thinks way too much of herself. She lives in lycra, carries a cheesy fixed grin on her face, and her livid bottle-blonde hair is permanently tied into a tight bun. Maddie and I don't get on.

'Now then. The Dance Festival. I have to submit the entries this week. You're here at half-term of course?'

There we go again. Manners! Some grown-ups need to remember a bit of respect. Like *'How are you, Abi? Feeling better now? Thanks for dropping by. Glass of anything?'*

'I think so,' I said tentatively, glowering at my feet.

'Naturally, I've got you down for tap and jazz solo classes. And I presume I can put you in for the intermediate ballet, and song and dance as well?' Everything about Ciarán is hard. Her grating voice, her dark little eyes, her taut muscles. There's not an ounce of spare flesh or kindness in her. 'I want to score every point we can over Bullen's.' She smiled maliciously.

'You're not *working*!' she yelled over her shoulder at the poor mites in the class. 'What's the point in just marking it? Stretch out. Go on… 5, 6, 7, 8, and turn and RUN! God help us!'

Even Maddie looked put out by this interjection. The dancers were clearly already working their little socks off.

Ciarán's Dance School and Bullen's Arts are the only establishments of their kind in south Leicester, the superpowers of the Midlands dance scene, daggers absolutely drawn. Ciarán and Miss Bullen simply hate each other. Points and prizes at the annual Dance Festival mean more six-year-old hopefuls through the front door of the successful outfit, and more students mean more fees. I'm not stupid. I can see how it works. The problem is, me, I like dancing. Just dancing, for the pure pleasure of feeling my body move to the music. I'm not remotely interested in dressing up or being a star or scoring points for anyone. And Ciarán is the lesser of two evils, 'cos Dora Bullen is worse than Ciarán, from what I've seen. When Bullen lost it at the festival two years ago, it gave a whole new meaning to throwing toys out of your pram. She didn't quite lie on the floor screaming, but it wasn't far short. And that was just because she disagreed with one of the adjudicator's placings.

'I'm not sure about the song and dance,' I tried. 'You've got lots of people better than me. What about Georgina and Alice?'

'Don't you worry about them, dear,' said Ciaran patronizingly. 'They'll be pulling their weight, you can be sure of that! I know you don't like song and dance, but really, you're much better than you think you are. Now, I've got a clown costume that would fit you beautifully, and we could do something nice and *adagio* to that lovely Sondheim tune. I don't *think* the song's too difficult for you…'

With these things it's always about palming you off with old and sweat-stained costumes that someone wore for an end of the pier show twenty years ago. It makes my flesh creep. As I thought about it, I felt myself give a little shudder.

'No,' I heard myself say, adenoidally, doing my Eddie Finn impression. The atmosphere in the studio was stifling, and I'd suddenly gone all bunged up. My head was throbbing. Who did she think she was? *'You're much better than you think you are! I don't think the song's too difficult!'* I pulled myself up to my full five feet one.

'I'll give the ballet a go, if you really think it's worth it, Ciarán, but I'm not doing song and dance for you this year. Sorry!'

She looked thunderstruck.

'Well!' was all she could say, arms in a double teapot of frustration and annoyance. 'Well!'

On the way home, I felt really proud of myself for standing up to her. I was walking at least two inches taller. And my head had suddenly stopped aching. I felt better than I had for days. But somehow I know I haven't heard the end of the wretched clown costume. Some day soon, it and Ciarán will be back and mad to get even.

Over Sunday lunch today, roast beef and apple pie, there was a 'What's been going on at school, Abi?' conversational moment from Dad.

I explained about the A Club, and joined up the dots for him on the Sam Saward-fest this Wednesday.

'About time,' he said.

I asked him to enlighten me.

'There's been too much of this dumbing-down,' he said aggressively. 'They've not been asking enough of you. Too much energy spent on trivia, and things you should have been doing in primary school.'

I don't know how Dad thinks he knows this, because it's Mum who always goes to parents' evenings, unless of course there's important stuff like school architecture to discuss, so at best it's all second-hand news to him. But I didn't get a chance to object, because Gran chimed in with her twopence worth.

'You see some of these girls walking up the road,' she said, and I knew immediately what was coming next. 'If they're wearing trousers you can see their pants peeking out over the top of them, and if they're wearing skirts, the skirts are hitched up so high you can practically see their pants from underneath. And they wonder why boys get the wrong idea. Now I ask you, what is the school thinking about? Even when *you* went to school, Mary, uniform meant uniform, didn't it? They'd have had the ruler out, to make sure your skirt was long enough. And woe betide you if it wasn't. Am I right or am I right?'

Mum's honest enough that she didn't go for that one. She and I have talked about this often, and her lot were no better than we are! Except they had an obsession with some group called the Bay City Rollers who were into a tartan thing, so Mum used to customize her uniform with scarves and bits of old kilts. Though clearly Gran never knew about that. Or has conveniently forgotten.

'Anyway,' said Dad, slightly embarrassed by the girly turn in the chat, 'it's the reason we moved here in the first place – to get you and Pete into Willowmede...'

No pressure then.

'... And I have to say, up to now, we've been wondering if it was a mistake. It didn't do much for Pete...'

'Gee, thanks Dad,' grunted big brother.

'... No, hear me out, son! What I was going to say was it seemed like it might be failing Abi too...'

'The A Club sounds a cool idea,' said Debs. 'I wish there'd been something like that when I was still in school...'

'I don't think advanced hairdressing's what they had in mind,' sniped Pete.

OK, years ago Debs had gone through a stage of wanting to be a hair designer, on her way to computer programming. Now she reached a hand across and tweaked his ear, the way I remember her doing when we were all much younger. And just as he used to do then, Pete squealed in pain. When Debs goes for you, she doesn't muck around.

'Children, behave!' said Mum, mock seriously. 'And that includes you, David. You started this!'

'All I'm saying is that it's a good thing they're seeking to raise Abi's expectations,' Dad continued gamely. 'And we need a lot more of it. Or society's in trouble. Big-time! It's the reason why there's chewing gum on the streets. And why all students think about is drinking and clubbing!'

He looked meaningfully at Pete, who raised his hands in a 'not me' fashion.

And just then, the phone rang. Talk about being saved by the bell. Except when Mum answered it, of all people, it was AD.

'It's for you,' Mum said to me, raising her eyebrows, after AD had clearly gone through a big apology routine.

'Teachers phoning on a Sunday,' Gran muttered very audibly. 'And at lunchtime too. Whatever next?'

I was trying to shake off images of AD and Hughesey canoodling on the sofa in Thornton Bramleigh.

'I'm so sorry to interrupt your lunch, Abi,' AD said, 'but I've just realized I'm going to be away Monday and Tuesday on a course, and though I think everything's more or less organized for Sam Saward and Wednesday evening, I wondered if you'd like to give the vote of thanks after the gig, on behalf of the A Club?'

Gig? What did AD think he was doing? Running Glastonbury?

'... Only, there should be some press there, Rosie Pickings from the *Examiner*, people like that, and we want to get things right, don't we? Maybe they'll even want some snaps of you and so on. I could have asked you on Wednesday but I thought you might like a bit of warning. How do you feel about that? OK?'

'Yeah, sure, no problem,' I said. The alien seemed to have returned to colonize my head. I hoped it liked sharing it with cold germs.

'That's wonderful!' enthused AD, 'And please apologize to your parents again for me. Look forward to seeing you on Wednesday then! Bye!'

And he rang off, probably to snog Zoe Hughes.

'Well?' asked Dad.

'Another reason to be cheerful,' I said.

There I was on Tuesday evening, chewing a pencil and trying to think of something witty to put in my thank-you speech for the Sam Saward thing, when my mobile chirruped. It was a text from Drew.

Problem, it read, *Cn U hlp?*

I sighed, and then immediately felt bad about it. But I mean, what was it going to be this time? The previous night we'd been on the phone for three-quarters of an hour about the causes of the Second World War, for heaven's sake. Life's too short. And on Saturday... Well, I can't even remember what it was, but there was something. Now Drew knows tons more about German rearmament and the League of Nations than I'll ever want to, but when it comes to putting stuff on paper or, like, making a decision about *anything*, the boy seems to have a problem. So I expect he picked up a bit of attitude from my carefully crafted reply...

Wot?

Thirty seconds later he texted.

Locked out!

Well at least that was different and conceivably entertaining, so I called him straight back. Maybe the break from pencil-chewing would give me some inspiration.

'Just tell me how!' I said, sounding like my mum already.

'It's easy to do,' he said a bit huffily. 'Went out for some fish'n'chips, let the front door slam shut, then remembered I'd left the keys on the kitchen table.'

Drew lives in a smart flat about half a mile away. Most things about Drew's family are smart. Smart jobs, smart clothes, smart BMWs (one each!). Just an idiot son!

'So where are your mum and dad?'

'Away overnight.'

'Uh-huh. Is that legal?'

'Some posh dinner at Dad's work.'

'That's not what I asked. When are they back, then?'

'Tomorrow evening. I think.'

'You *think*?'

'Yeah, yeah, tomorrow evening. Look, whatever! What do I do, Abi?'

'Stay over at our place?'

'No good. I've left the oven on,' Drew whinged pathetically. 'And there's Cassandra…'

Their overweight, over-spoiled cat. I boggled at the thought of Drew cooking. This was an entirely new insight.

'The oven?'

'I was going to warm up a Tesco's apple pie.'

So not actually cooking.

'Just give me a moment. I'll call you back,' I said, realizing this was a real crisis of a small sort. 'Maybe Pete can help.'

I knocked on Pete's door. For once he was in, and not down the pub.

'What do *you* want?' he said.

'Is that nice?'

'Well, you wouldn't have knocked otherwise, would you?'

Bang to rights. I explained, and pleaded, and eventually he hauled himself off his bed, with Pete's trademark world-weary *'Let me sort out your problem, little girl'* sigh. The vanity of blokes!

'You're a real star, Pete,' I breathed. Insincere flattery gets you everywhere with my bro.

We found Drew hopping from foot to foot outside the building where his flat was.

'Apart from anything else, I need to go to the toilet,' he said.

'What do we do, Pete?' I asked.

'Well, there's a hedge over there. No one'll see!'

'I didn't mean *that*. About getting in!'

'Watch and learn, dudes,' Pete said annoyingly. 'Watch and learn!'

We trooped up the stairs to the flat's front door. Pete produced a plastic card from his wallet, brandished it in front of us like a magician with a stage prop, and started woggling it around in the crack of the door by the lock. We watched, and learned... zilch! The door stayed resolutely locked. After five minutes, admiration and hope began to fade. Five minutes after *that* and, with his amazing magic powers still not working, the magician himself was losing his cool. Good thing it wasn't a glamorous assistant being cut in half, or worse, being reassembled.

'Well, it's worked every other time,' he said.

'So just how many times have you done this?' I asked incredulously. He ignored me.

'No good,' he pronounced, like it was a final thing. He stood up and looked accusingly at Drew. 'Lock won't budge an inch. Don't you guys ever oil it?'

Drew resumed his war dance to the toilet gods.

We went back down the stairs, and studied the outside of the building.

'Isn't that your front room?' I said, pointing at a first floor window with a sash which was very slightly ajar.

'Yeah. So?'

'Well, all we need is a ladder...'

'And someone to climb it...' said Drew quickly.

I looked at Pete.

'Pete's good with heights,' I said. 'He goes rock climbing. Don't you, Pete?'

'Yeah,' said big brother. 'But we don't *have* a ladder, do we?'

Luckily Mr Protheroe, who lives in the house across the road from Drew's flat, did. Mr Protheroe is one of those well-scrubbed, well-organized OAPs you see at flower shows or at church, with a tanned and weathered face and a shiny bald patch on top of his head you could probably use as a Sky telly receiver. His garage looked like the local branch of B&Q, drawers full of screws and nails, racks of wood and tools. A ladder was no problem, but we were sent off with strict instructions not to break it or there'd be trouble. How do you break a metal ladder?

We propped it up against the wall of the flat, and dug its legs into the earth of a flower bed. The ladder reached to the window, just about, but now it came to it, Pete didn't look too certain about the prospect of the ascent.

'It's all right for you, kid,' he said. 'A bit of respect! When I'm climbing a mountain, I'm tied on and I can't fall off. I'm on my own here!'

'I'll go if you like,' Drew's small voice volunteered gamely. He was probably thinking of the bathroom. Why do boys find willpower in this respect more difficult than girls? Weaklings!

Pete gathered himself to his full five foot ten, metaphorically hitched up his braces, and said, 'It's OK, Drew, stay cool. I'm the man.'

He actually said that. Can you believe it?

Gingerly, he began to climb the rungs. From the look on his face I knew he was scared witless.

Pete had just reached the top and was tugging awkwardly on the window sash, trying to raise it a few inches, when the distant Dopplering sound of a police siren came suddenly and ominously closer. With a roar of engine and squeal of brakes a fuzz-wagon screeched to a halt beside us and Mr Protheroe's ladder. Drew and I looked at each other, pupils dilating, guilty without reason. Neighbourhood Watch clearly worked better here than it did in our street. Or perhaps Mr Protheroe was having a little joke? Pete, startled by the noise, half turned to look and wobbled dangerously, grabbing at the ledge with one hand. For a heart-stopping moment I thought we were going to need the assistance of a second emergency service, but though the metal ladder juddered, he managed to steady himself and hold on.

'So exactly what's going on here then, young lady?' said the policeman, climbing out of the car and pulling on his cap. His female companion stayed put, radioing into base to describe how they'd caught another violent criminal gang red-handed. A powerful waft of sickly sweet aftershave followed the bloke out of the car. All I could think was *Fancy being stuck all day in a car with that! Chemical warfare or what!*

After a dodgy ninety seconds they believed us of course, because luckily Drew had his library card and other stuff which proved he really did live at Flat 3 Ransome House. And I guess neither Pete nor I fitted the profile of your regular Leicester crims. Then, when Pete had assured them of his climbing club credentials, they watched in a concerned fashion as he made a second ascent of the ladder, this time successfully manoeuvring himself through the window to open the front door.

What was slightly less wonderful was that, after Drew had streaked into the flat like a dingbat to relieve the pressure, emerging from the bathroom like someone whose life had suddenly taken a big turn for the better, Starsky and Mrs Hutch started on the third degree about his parents' whereabouts.

'No older brothers and sisters?' asked the female copper.

'They do this a lot, then?' chuntered the bloke PC. 'Leaving you alone in the house?' He cast a disapproving eye around the Chapples' high-tech kitchen which in Drew's one evening home alone had acquired a lived-in look, scattered with textbooks, papers and cat litter.

'No one you could stay with tonight, is there?' said the woman.

I began to think Drew might end up with Social Services or something stupid, so a quick call to Mum later, it was agreed Drew would spend the night on our sofa after all.

Back at Chateau Goodenough, Drew started to beat himself up over a mug of cocoa before bed.

'Mum and Dad are going to go mental,' he said woefully.

'Could have happened to anyone,' I lied. Drew is definitely more forgetful than the average person, but this wasn't the moment for painful honesty.

'These kinds of things are always happening to me,' he moaned. 'Dad's always telling me I'm going to waste my life if I'm not careful. He's probably right, too!'

Extraordinary. It must be a father-son thing. My dad sometimes carries on at Pete like this, though he's never tried it out on me. But

48

if that's what Drew gets all the time, it's no wonder he's got zilcho confidence when it comes to school.

'Look,' I said, 'You can't do anything about it now. Worry about it tomorrow. All because of you, Drew Chapple, I haven't written anything for this vote of thanks thingy to Sam Saward, so get your thinking cap on, and tell me some brilliant stuff to say. Right then. Let's go!'

The following evening at seven fifteen, almost everything was peachy for the A Club's inaugural event in Willowmede's brand spanking new Judi Dench Theatre. There was a podium. There was one of those clever autocue things so Sam Saward could look sincere while he read his words of wisdom. There was a single powerful lamp focusing a pool of brilliant white light around where Saint Sam would stand. And there were enough flowers to start a florist's business cascading over the stage into the audience. Yes sir, half the school might be falling down, but our new theatre looked fantastic. One day, we might even be allowed to do some drama there. But only if we promise not to make the place untidy!

There were swanky plush maroon tip-up seats, a state-of-the-art sound system, amazing lights and a proper green room, all thanks to the mighty financial muscle of Logic Solutions, sponsors of the new, improved Willowmede Academy. And, surprise, surprise, there, hanging above the podium, was Logic Solutions' nasty yellow company logo clashing horrendously with the décor.

To one side of the stage a large screen was suspended. On it was printed the words:

BIG ON WINNING?
THEN GET:
BIG ON PREPARATION
BIG ON POTENTIAL
BIG ON PEOPLE
BIG ON PROFILE
= BIG ON PERFORMANCE

The theatre was slowly filling up. We A Clubbers buzzed about, smiling and handing out programmes featuring the slightly hyper-real, smarmy picture of Sam Saward's toothy grin, and another reminder, as if anyone could forget it, that what we were there for was to learn *HOW TO WIN BIG*. Big Ben, AD and Zoe Hughes were meeting and greeting, schmoozing anyone important. The mayor was there, rattling his chains. There was a foxy-faced little woman with red hair I recognized as Audrey Pearson, the local MP. From the way he was pointing at the Logic Solutions logo, and pumping Big Ben's hand, I guessed the fat bloke in the shiny suit was probably the company's Managing Director, now Willowmede's new Chair of Governors. A photographer was snapping away as people arrived, and the young woman with spiky hair, rather too high heels and a 'look at me' fuschia top showing a lot of tanned bosom, was probably the *Examiner*'s Rosie Pickings.

As I say, almost everything was peachy. Except. Except, where was Sam Saward?

Apparently, he'd first rung at about six o'clock, to say he'd left Manchester a bit late, and not to worry if he didn't show at Willowmede until seven. Then AD had fielded a call at about quarter to seven saying SS was stuck in a motorway traffic jam, but it was OK 'cos he'd got Sat Nav in the Porsche Cayenne and his personal assistant was now taking a route via the back roads. I know this because I overheard AD say, 'Personal assistant? Sat Nav? A Porsche Cayenne?', like he was dead impressed. Probably thinking he was in the wrong job. No Porsche Cayennes in the Willowmede teachers' car park during a normal week!

'Not "Big on Punctuality" then?' Em smirked in my ear.

It was fun watching AD hopping about about like Drew in need of the lavatory when he thought no one was looking, while in public trying very hard not to spook Big Ben or any of the VIPs. But by 7.20, AD's head was in his hands, and Hughesey was unashamedly offering words of comfort intimately in one ear.

'Sweet!' murmured Em. 'Don't they make a lovely pair?'

'*You* know about them too?'

50

'Doesn't everyone?'

Drew, who clearly didn't, interrupted their one-to-one with, 'Sir? What are you going to do, sir?'

The wild look in AD's eyes suggested he hadn't got a clue. He smoothed back his hair, rubbed the back of his neck a few times, and stared briefly into the distance. Then he laughed. Rather a manic laugh, but a laugh nonetheless.

'Do you know, Drew, I haven't got the foggiest?' And he laughed again. 'Like the old song says, "Whatever will be, will be". Every problem's an opportunity, so they say...'

Hughesey looked concerned. Her man was under pressure. And maybe cracking.

7.30 arrived and still no Sam Saward, then 7.35. The natives in the theatre were getting restless. The audience noise level was rising noticeably. Vivaldi's *Four Seasons* were drowning under the chatter. Another ten minutes and there'd be a chorus of another old song: 'Why are we waiting?'

At 7.38, AD leapt into action.

'Right!' he said decisively, and took off down to the front row where Big Ben was sitting with Logic Solutions' boss. From the back of the theatre, we saw AD whispering in Big Ben's ear, and there was a lot of nodding and shaking of heads. Then, as AD moved up onto the stage and towards the spare microphone, Mr Logic Solutions stood in embarrassed fashion, buttoning his jacket, and shuffling his feet.

'Oh God, what a balls-up!' Drew stage-whispered, loud enough that the back rows could hear. A few parents turned round and tutted.

Zoe Hughes shot him a look designed to kill. The sound system boomed and squeaked into business.

'Good evening, everyone, and welcome to the Judi Dench Theatre on this, Willowmede's very first public event here. I'm afraid Sam Saward has been unavoidably delayed, so, before he arrives, I'd like to welcome on stage Bryan Fortescue, Managing Director of Logic Solutions, to tell us...'

But simultaneously there was the sound of a banging door and a commotion at the side of the stage. A tall, expensively suited figure with a toothy smile could be seen suddenly lurking in the wings. At 7.44 precisely, the cavalry had arrived to save AD's wobbling reputation, and creakily bring the A Club into official existence. Mr Logic Solutions sat down again, looking doubly embarassed to have been sold such a gigantic dummy. Big Ben looked daggers at AD while Sam Saward strode forward to the podium. There was some half-hearted clapping. Big Ben decided it wasn't good enough, so he stood and conducted the applause, turning and demanding that the audience give SS a hero's welcome.

'Big in a Porsche,' giggled Em under her breath.

'Big on porridge,' echoed Drew. From the size of Sam Saward's paunch, his rugby-*playing* days were well behind him.

'Big in trousers,' Em chorused, in danger of helplessness.

Zoe Hughes put a warning finger to her lips, and shook her head vigorously. I pretended they were nothing to do with me.

I couldn't tell you now exactly what Sam Saward said, except that he told lots of stories about how he and the England rugby team had won the World Cup, and were the best players ever. But was it just me or were all the stories designed to show how clever SS was? He certainly mentioned his book every other minute. Still, everyone seemed to think he was very funny and laughed a lot. Me too. I suppose you get carried along with it all, don't you? Char had been quiet earlier on, but now she gazed adoringly at her hero, hanging on every word he said, and I just knew her one aim of the evening was to get the bloke's autograph. Or possibly a telephone number.

In the end, the message seemed to come down to working hard and believing in yourself. Big deal. I thought everyone knew that, but perhaps they don't.

My knees were knocking and and my heart was thumping when I walked down with my bit of paper to give the vote of thanks. No autocue for me.

'*Big* it up, girl,' chortled Em as she pushed me off down the aisle.

Immediately I got this weird, suspicious idea into my head that Em might have stuck something stupid on the back of my Willowmede sweatshirt, like – I don't know – a note saying 'Kick me!' or something. And the longer I was up there on stage, the more convinced I was she'd really done it. So I know I stood there awkwardly, looking like a real dork, but at any rate most of the words came out in the right order, and when I finished off by saying (with a well-rehearsed smile) that I was sure all of us would try to be *big* performers in future, there was a *big* round of applause which made me feel better. And I saw Big Ben and Mr Logic beaming broadly and nodding their heads, so I suppose it must have been all right.

'Creep,' said Em when I was beside her again at the back. 'Lick, lick, grovel grovel. You're a dead cert to be Head Girl, already so soon. But I'll still like you. Provided you remember to do what I want.'

The way she said it was a bit sharp. *Miaow*, I thought.

'Did you stick something on my back?' I asked.

'You what? Crazy woman!'

Then came the photographs. Us with SS and Big Ben. AD with SS and Big Ben. Us with AD, and so on and so on.

Actually, Rosie Pickings is really nice. What with the fuschia blouse and the cleavage and all that, I expected her to be really up herself, but she was friendly and normal, like one of us. Drew, Em and me chatted to her about the A Club, and what we were going to do. She didn't take notes, just recorded what we said into an MP3 gizmo, which I thought was cool. Rosie says there'll be something in the *Examiner* on Monday. Can't wait!

Monday lunchtime, Em and I were deputed by the other A Clubbers to go and pick up the day's edition of the *Examiner* from Mr Fernando's corner shop.

Mr Fernando's a bit of a character, if you know what I mean. He's very small and wizened and dark and he was born in Sri Lanka where it rains a lot, as he never stops telling people when they complain about the British weather. 'You think this is rain? I'm telling you, this is not rain. You come to Colombo, and I will show you real rain. Six, nine, twelve inches in one day!'

His eyes lit up when he saw us.

'Hello, my very good friends Emily and Abigail. How nice that you always bring the sunshine with you. And how are you today?'

We told him we were well, and could we buy an *Examiner* please.

'Ah, yes!' said Mr Fernando. 'Very interesting. The paper tells me good things. No longer will I have to worry about Willowmede students when they come to my shop. Never again will I have to chase them off my premises for stealing or being cheeky. From now on they will all be kind and polite, just like Emily and Abigail.'

We said we hoped so, and, intrigued, escaped with our copy of the *Examiner*, resisting the temptation to read it there and then. Well, I would have done actually, but Em snatched it away before I had the chance.

'Bit keen, aren't we Abs, to see our ugly big mug in print? Didn't your mum teach you patience was a virtue? Don't want you getting too big for your boobs, do we?'

Interesting. Just like on Wednesday evening, she was winding me up. I ignored her. Em can be like that sometimes. But wouldn't she have been the same, if it had been *her* 'ugly mug' on show?

The front page promised that pages six and seven would tell us all about the visit of 'England rugby hero Sam Saward'. But it wasn't the day's biggest story. Oh no! That was 'Thugs Bunny', all about rabbits who'd supposedly started terrorizing humans in some faraway Leicestershire village on account of being high on a diet of magic mushrooms. The rabbits, not the humans! Or so some mad person was claiming.

That's the good old *Examiner* for you. It can be a fun read. Better than Dad's boring *Daily Telegraph* and not as filthy as the rags Pete likes to look at. It's good to know what's going on in your town. But you've got to take it with a pinch of salt.

We laid the paper out on a table in the hall in between our sandwiches. The A Clubbers plus a few other people crowded round. Page six was mostly an interview with Sam Saward, his exploits in New Zealand with the rugby team, stuff about his book, and how he still managed to find time to run a business *and* have a wife and three kids. Mr Superman, then! Funny, he hadn't looked very married to me. Something about the way his personal assistant hung about just *too* close to his shoulder reminded me of AD and Zoe Hughes.

Page seven was the Willowmede bit. A headline ran: 'Academy thinking big for high-fliers', by 'Examiner Education Reporter, Rosie Pickings'. We all cheered because yes, there was a picture of us looking cheesily at Sam Saward, and also one of me doing my podium thing with SS in the background picking his nose and eating it. Well, that's what Em suggested. Me, I thought it was more of a scratch than a pick. I didn't look *completely* stupid, and if there ever had been a notice saying 'Kick me' on my back, it had fallen off by then, but the photographer *had* caught me with my mouth wide open. It looked more like I was *singing* thank you to SS than saying it!

Why am I always the odd one out? No one else around the table seemed to see anything wrong with Rosie's article. True, most of it was perfectly innocuous stuff, though we couldn't recognize any of the things we'd actually said to her written anywhere. But you know that prickly feeling you get up the back of your neck when you've been caught out, or you gradually realize something bad, like scoring low in a test when you were sure you'd hit the max? Well, the further down the page I read, the more I got that exact feeling. The others were busy teasing Char about getting Sam the Man's autograph.

'You *do* fancy him, don't you?' Em was going. 'You'd unpack his bags any day, you would!' And there was more not-in-front-of-Grandma stuff about inflating rugby balls etc etc. You can write the gags for yourself.

All the time, Char was going, 'Shut up, Em' and blushing furiously, just so there couldn't be any doubt about how star-struck she was, while I was thinking to myself, *This is weird. What on earth is Rosie Pickings up to?*

Drew spotted I'd gone quiet, and asked, 'Everything OK, Abs?'

'Well, see what you think!' I answered. I pointed at some paragraphs printed towards the bottom of the page under the title 'The *Examiner* comments…'

'*As a Comprehensive School, Willowmede can perhaps be best described as having a chequered history.* Examiner *readers will probably remember some of its less happy times. Three years ago, before the appointment of its current head teacher Mr Ben Browning, we reported that for the third year in a row Willowmede was firmly anchored near the bottom of all its league tables and in danger of being placed under special measures.*

'*Over the years,* Examiner *readers have also expressed their anxieties about ongoing inter-school feuding between Willowmede and Ratcliffe schools which in 2001 infamously led to a number of arrests in the course of a riot on the Harcourt Estate.*

'*Ex-pupils of Willowmede include convicted bank robber, Sean Williams, and Sophie-Jane Tyler, currently languishing in a Thai gaol on drug-smuggling charges.*

'*Staff and pupils are quoted as saying that with the renaming of the school as Willowmede Academy, under its new Logic Solutions-led governing body, this unfortunate past has been put firmly behind them. The* Examiner *can only applaud their optimistic spirit and wish them well! Our city needs schools of quality and vision. Then maybe Britain can be world-beaters in more than just rugby!'*

'What's wrong with that?' said Drew. 'Seems fine to me.'

'You don't think it's a bit... snidey? Knocking the school like that?' I asked. 'I thought Rosie was just supposed to be reporting on Wednesday night, not writing a shock horror exposé.'

'It's probably all true,' said Sally Kennedy. 'I remember my dad talking about that bloke Sean Williams. He met him in a club once. Said he was a really nasty piece of work.'

'I remember the bundle with Ratcliffe,' intoned Eddie. 'Gory, man!' Everyone looked at him expectantly, hoping for some more juicy details. But that was it.

'She's right about the league table thing,' Drew resumed. 'My parents didn't really want to send me here because of that...'

'Anyway,' said Char, 'it doesn't say Rosie Pickings wrote that stuff. It just says ' "The *Examiner* comments..." '

'I know, but...' I began. I was about to say 'you could probably dig up that kind of dirt on any school you wanted', when Em suddenly started on me. I was shocked. It came out of the clear blue sky, an assault more than a wind-up.

'Oh, leave it out, Abs!' she said. 'What does it matter, anyway? It's just words. Nobody believes what they read in the papers. Some of us have had it with your attitude, y'know. It's like you're worried going to a slightly crap school might damage your precious rep.'

As I was reeling from the attack, AD strolled by. I don't know if he realized Em and I were in the process of falling out, but he asked casually, 'Everything OK?'

'Yes, sir,' we chorused dutifully.

'Seen the paper, sir?' Char asked enthusiastically.

'Yeah,' AD drawled. A bit guarded, I thought, so I pressed him.

'What did you think of it, sir?'

AD paused, furrowing his brow like he was turning the whole heat of his awesome brainpower on the question. For a moment, it seemed like there'd be a great utterance, but then he thought better of it. All he finally said was, 'Hmm. Yeah. Interesting...' And he strolled on, smiling an enigmatic smile.

I didn't say 'Told you so' to Em, but that's what I thought. Obviously, AD felt the same as me. And Em? Well, it was blindingly obvious she was just jealous, wasn't she? There couldn't be any other explanation.

All Tuesday, Em stayed out of my way, or was rudely offhand when we couldn't actually avoid being in the same place at the same time. But by Wednesday break, I thought this really couldn't go on, so I lit the peace pipe and suggested, 'Hey Em, fancy going bowling tomorrow night?'

I knew I ought really to be at the church youth group (this would be the second week running I'd missed Tomorrow's People) but right now, Em and me staying mates had to be the priority.

At first she was grudgingly like, 'Yeah, all right. If you want...', which was Em knowing she was in the wrong but not wanting to admit it. I resisted the temptation to say, 'Look, you ungrateful cow, I'm putting myself in the bad with Jana because of you!'

Then she went, 'Don't you think we should invite Char?' which missed the point entirely. Then again, it might just have been Em being thoughtful in a warped sort of way, so of course I gave her the benefit of the doubt and said, yes, sure! And then I found myself saying, which was true (the return of the alien?), that there weren't any A Club meetings during the week, and perhaps we should invite the other A Clubbers along for a bit of bonding, ha ha, i.e. Drew, Sally, Eddie and Sylvester. Well that's who the A Club is right now, though there are a couple of don't-knows hanging around, trying to decide whether we're sufficiently cool to be worth their valuable time.

Em's turn to be surprised! The way she looked at me so brain-dead, I guess she wished she'd thought of that and was annoyed because she hadn't. Nevertheless, she mumbled a crabby, croaked 'OK!', and so there I was, suddenly stuck with making a major event work at twenty-four hours' notice rather than patching things up with my best buddy, and thinking to myself, *How did that happen then?*

'We'll need two cars,' I said to Em. 'Any chance your mum'd help out?'

'Haven't got a clue,' she answered, morosely unhelpful.

'OK. Whatever. I'll find a way,' I chuntered, down on myself and her. If you want something done, find a busy person, blah, blah! The bowling alley's situated in an out of town shopping centre, i.e. the developers who built it know they're forcing people to travel miles for their bit of fun, and hope they'll stop off for the weekly food shopping and a McDonald's while they're there. Clever, but twisted. Anyway, the point is, it's too far for anyone to walk.

I tried Drew about the car thing. He looked at his watch, as if that was relevant, and said in an absent-minded way that meant any answer he gave couldn't be trusted, 'Yeah, should be OK.'

'And you can tell me definitely when?'

'Tonight?' he answered vaguely.

Well, it was something.

By the end of the lunch hour I'd tracked down the others. Sylvester looked completely delighted to be asked. I could have hugged him for just saying, 'Yeah! Great!' No hassle. No complaints. I didn't bother him or Char about the transport. I thought it was probably an issue with Char's parents right now, and I hadn't a clue about Sylvester's folk, except he doesn't live far from Willowmede, so I figured him getting home wouldn't be too difficult.

Sally looked pleased too. 'I can probably twist Beth's arm to pick me up,' she said, like I should know who Beth was. Dad's girlfriend? Older sister?

I cornered Eddie by the lockers, and when I said 'Hi!', he ducked his head like I'd tried to cuff him round the ear. Sometimes frogs jump through the open back door into the Goodenough house, and one of us has to catch them and gently put them back by the pond. Snaring Eddie reminded me of that. Mental note: always speak quietly when confronting the greater-spotted Eddie. Frogs, dogs, tortoises: it's always animals that come to mind when dealing with that boy.

I explained about the bowling.

'What d'you think?' I asked.

He shrugged.

'Go on! It'll be a laugh,' I tried. 'The others are all up for it.'

'Dunno. What time, then?'

'We need you,' I said, really turning the screws. 'Drew and Sylvester need you. Otherwise it'll be too much of a girly night.'

His eyes finally turned up at me from under the hair, cautious, questioning. Everything about Eddie was tense, like he'd scuttle away if he could see the slightest opening or excuse. And then the obvious dawned on me, like a slap round the face. This was a lack-of-readies problem, wasn't it? Here I was, waving something nice in front of Eddie, but it was something he probably couldn't afford. So, fool that I am, I said,

'Don't worry about the money. We won't play much, and we can always split the costs. It's you being there that's important. Really!'

'OK,' was the most I could get out of him. Not the flicker of a smile. No 'That's brilliant! Thank you so much! How kind!'

'That's a yes, is it, then, Eddie?'

'Yeah. S'pose so.'

Aaaargh!

Miracle of miracles, the bowling thing worked just fine. Diaries and watches were synchronized. Transport was organized. Parents were squared (or in Eddie's case, possibly ignored). And we had a really good time. I'd been joking with Em about the bonding thing, but on Thursday, for the first time, the A Club felt like a group. There was warmth and friendship. We were a team.

Amazingly, Em and I managed to call a truce, and were nicer to each other than we'd been all week. Char was laughing, which was good to see. Sally was good fun. When you get to know her, she's not half so forbidding. She's got a quiet, sideways sense of humour I really like. Sylvester was quiet, but stunned us all by the fact that he knew everyone's scores in his head without ever looking at the screens. Like Char had said, his head for figures is totally spooky.

Complete recall, and instant calculation.

Drew was convinced he'd easily be the champion bowler, and gave out that the rest of us weren't really fit to share a lane with him. Thank you God, but it turned out that not only was Char a far better bowler than Drew (strikes and spares all over the place), but so was Eddie. To look at him, you'd think Eddie wouldn't have the strength to propel anything bigger than a ping-pong ball down the lane. Cartoon-style, I expected him to turn head over heels and end up with the skittles down the far end. But he gave Char a good run for her (our!) money, while Drew was nowhere, back with the bowling drongoes like me and Em.

'It's my wrist,' he moaned, clutching said part of his anatomy. 'Been playing up all week!'

Yeah, right!

There was a moment towards the end of our hour at the alley, when I sat back with my lime and lemonade, and looked at the A Club strutting its stuff, laughing and joking, even Eddie, and felt so pleased with myself. I'd *made* the evening happen, and it felt good. Why can't every day be fun like that?

On the back of Thursday evening's positive vibe, I zinged my way through Friday and Saturday. Which was good, because there were grown-ups on the prowl everywhere.

AD had got wind that the A Club had taken itself off for the evening, and he was so made up, you'd have thought it was his idea.

'Great stuff, Abi,' he enthused. 'Keep it up. Mr Browning's thrilled with the way things are going.'

Well, just so long as Big Ben was happy, what more could we ask!

Penny had another go about German and next year.

'You've got flair, Abi. A natural talent for languages. Such a pity if it went to waste...' he was going. Yeah, yeah, yeah.

'Thank you, sir,' I said, smiling as angelically as I knew how.

It's a bummer. I can't tell him what I really think, 'cos it'll turn him into a mortal enemy. Which I definitely do not need. How long can I stall him?

Everard's been hunting me down because of my irregular appearances at rehearsals for her *Requiem,* and I've bought *her* off by registering a late entry in the solo violin section of the music and dance fest. It's on the same morning as the jazz dance for Ciaran, so no skin off my nose, if it keeps her quiet. There are only four people entered in the class, so despite my nasty fiddle technique, there's even the outside chance of winning something.

Talking of Ciarán, she was actually pleasant to me on Saturday, and said she thought I was dancing well at the moment. Which, considering what I was doing thoughout half of Friday night (as you'll shortly hear!), was entirely remarkable.

I was checking myself out in the mirror the other day, like you do, and reckon I've grown an inch or two these past few months, which helps me look less like a pixie and more like a dancer. And if I stick it out, and pull in hard underneath, I can almost pretend I've got a chest worthy of mention. Happiness would be a B-cup!

I dropped in to see Jana before the church music group on Friday. I thought I owed her, what with missing Tomorrow's People the previous night. Feeling I was on a roll, I tackled her about the naffness of the name.

'That's what's wrong with church,' I said. 'It always sounds and looks like it belongs to yesterday.'

She raised a single eyebrow.

'I wish you'd been at the bowling alley, Jana!' I continued. 'Everyone wanted to be there, because they *knew* it would be *fun.* What do you think they'd say if I invited them to St Michael's?'

'Fun's the most important thing then, is it?' asked Jana.

Whoa! I could see where that was going.

'Not fair!' I said. 'Trick question.'

'Yeah, Jesus was so good with those,' she smiled, teasingly. Jana is *very* difficult to argue with.

'OK, let's put it this way,' I said. 'If the church sounds boring or out of date, it's not giving itself much of a chance, is it?'

'You might be right,' Jana conceded, and then would you believe it, changed the subject. One-eighty degrees. No messing. 'So tell me

Abi, how are you? Really?'

'I'm fine,' I said. 'I'm really fine. Why do you want to know? And look, why are you dodging the question? Do you know how annoying that is?'

'I just wondered,' she said. 'Haven't seen you for a while, have I? Not to talk to. Stuff happens. I get out of date.'

Which just left me feeling guilty. I tried to persuade her back to talking about the name thing, but she wouldn't have it, and I went off to choir practice feeling well dischuffed. Grown-ups always get the last word, always control the agenda. But hey, that's their problem. We're the future. We just have to keep fixing their mess, sooner or later.

I'd literally just walked through the door on Friday evening after choir, about half past eight, when the phone rang, and Mum shouted through from the kitchen, 'For you Abi!' There was that little edge to her voice, like it was someone she didn't want to hear from. And as she handed the phone over, she pulled an odd face, as if to say, 'What's this one all about, then?'

It was Char. Well, I *thought* it was Char. The voice was Char-like, but grunged-up and vague.

'It was... It was great lasht night, Abs,' she said, gushingly. 'I just wanted to tell you... It wash fantash... fantashtic!'

There seemed to be a lot of static on the phone line.

'Thanks, Char,' I said. 'That means a lot! It *was* good, wasn't it?'

'I had... I jusht had the most wunnerful time. I jusht...'

There was a gap in the flow. Like about thirty seconds' gap.

'Char? Char, are you still there?' I prompted. There was a sigh at Char's end, like she was getting sleepy, but no proper reply. Eventually she slurred, 'I jusht wanted you to know that... OK?'

Now I'm not a great expert on this kind of thing, but it didn't take a mastermind to work out that this was a drunk person.

'Anyway. That'sh all I wanted to shay,' she continued unsteadily. There was another long pause. 'I'm going to go now...'

'No, don't,' I said hurriedly. 'Don't you dare! Just stay on the line for a moment. Char, is anyone else there with you?'

'No,' she answered slowly. 'They've all... They've all gone out.'

'Yeah, OK, I've got that. And when will they be back, Char?'

'Oh, later. Later. Sometime later... much later!'

I must live in a *very* untypical household. My parents never go out. Well, once in a blue moon, maybe. But they have never, and I mean never, left me on my own overnight, or even for a whole evening in the house alone. But first Drew. Now Charlotte. Are these people stupid?

Not quite knowing what to do, I eventually rang off, making an excuse to Char and telling her I was going to call her back in five minutes. I quickly explained the situation to Mum, who was amazingly sensible. As she often is, to be fair.

'Debs is at home tonight,' she said. 'Give her a ring. She'll probably help you out. She knows a thing or two about hangovers!'

Debs was a complete and utter star. In fifteen minutes, she'd finished washing her hair, abandoned her plans for the evening and made it from her flat to our front door. Before you could say 'kitchen towels and J-cloths', we were driving off to Thornton Bramleigh in Debs' luminously yellow, microscopically small Japanese car. I rang Char to say we were on our way.

'Oh,' she said, 'That'sh nice!'

'I hope she isn't going to puke up *too* much,' Debs said. 'I've just had a bath!'

I don't have much to compare it with because I'm glad to say none of my friends have ever got drunk before, but the puke-factor seemed quite high enough to me.

Judging by what we eventually saw laid out on the occasional table in the Ellisons' lounge, Char had tried out the whole range of stuff from her parents' drinks cabinet. Some of the bottles were vaguely familiar, and others were colours and shapes I'd definitely never seen before. Like, have you heard of Blue Curaçao? Whatever, it's a great colour. When it's in the bottle and before it goes into the human body, that is.

I was pretty pleased with myself for being able to navigate Debs straight to the Ellisons' house. And getting in wasn't a problem either. No ladders needed. All we had to do was walk through a side passage and straight in through the back door.

Just before we pulled on the door handle, Debs said, 'You're sure this *is* Char's house?' and like you do, I had a sudden moment of panic. With no confidence at all, I said, 'I *think* so...'

So we called a nervous hello or two from the kitchen, and for a few seconds, all we could hear was the hum of the refrigerator while we looked nervously at each other, but then there came a soft answering groan. We found Char slumped on the lounge sofa, with a pile of books open on the floor around her, and a selection of drink as described at eye level on the table in front of her. Her eyes were glazed, and her face was generally an unnatural ivory colour.

'Hi!' she said weakly. 'How are you? It'sh nice to see you.' She made a feeble effort to move, but then gave up.

'We're fine,' said Debs briskly. 'I'm Debs, Abi's big sister. Listen to me, Charlotte, I need you to tell me. You haven't taken any pills with all this booze, have you?'

Even through the general glazedness, Char looked puzzled. 'Pills? Pills! No, I haven't taken any pills,' she muttered vaguely. 'Jusht... Jusht some coronation chicken.'

'Oh good,' said Debs wryly.

Then Char said, 'I don't feel very well.' And she struggled to get up.

'Washing-up bowl. Kitchen. Now,' Debs snapped at me. Then a second or so later, 'Too late! Oh well, we'll catch it next time.'

And we did. And the time after that too. But as a result of Char's first throw-up, the carpet wasn't looking good, and the sofa had suffered slightly too. Good thing we'd brought the J-cloths.

Eventually, there was nothing left for Char to bring up, so we carefully helped her up to bed. She was wearing a baggy t-shirt which seemed to have avoided the vomit, so we hauled off her jeans, covered her up, and left her to snore, while we went back downstairs and cleaned up the lounge as best we could.

'So what do we do now?' asked Debs.

I hadn't got a clue. We didn't have a key to lock up with, and it didn't seem like a cool idea to leave Char inside an unlocked house in that state. But what if no Ellison parent showed all night? Were we going to camp out in Thornton Bramleigh till the morning? And what if they did come home, and found strangers in their front room? I began to stop feeling sorry for Char and start feeling angry.

'Well it's just on eleven now,' said Debs. 'Why don't we give it till midnight. If they haven't come back by then, we might have to put Char in the car and take her back with us. I'll pull the Nissan into the drive, so they'll expect someone else to be here. I shouldn't think many housebreakers drive bright yellow microscopics!'

I had a feeling of déjà vu – you know, like you've been there before? I just hoped that if the cops arrived, they'd be different ones than those who'd turned up at Drew's pad!

At twelve, we decided to give it an extra half hour, since there was plenty of reading material to keep us amused, and we were warm enough on account of the Ellisons' super-efficient central heating. And, as it turned out, that was the right decision because at a quarter past midnight, Mrs Ellison arrived, and on her own.

Mrs E didn't look great either. Her hair was a mess, her clothes were pretty scruffy, and she was wearing next to no make-up. Her eyes were puffy, and the lines on her forehead looked like an advert for Botox – before treatment! I'd assumed Char's pa and ma had left her to go out on the town, but apparently not so.

But let's be positive here. Though it was obviously a shock for her to walk in and find strangers sprawled round her lounge, Mrs E took it surprisingly well. But then, when she'd got the basics of the story, and assured herself that Char wasn't dead but only sleeping, she simply said, 'I think you should go now.' Just that. No 'Thank you!'. No relieved smile. No small talk. She just wanted us out of her house. And so off we toddled home, me scratching my head, and Debs ranting about 1) Mrs E's ungratefulness and 2) her lack of common sense in leaving Char with nothing but the contents of an off-licence for company.

'What are these people on?' Debs said, more than once, flogging the gearstick into submission. 'It's enough to drive you to drink!'

Well, yeah, but no, but yeah!

Blog the Sixth
16 October

I've got into the habit of scribbling these blogs either side of Sunday lunch, so my last one missed the next chapter in *The Amazing Adventures of Char*. You'd better believe it. It gets more extraordinary by the minute.

Whoa, hold the front page, Abs! Exactly who do you think you are? The new Rosie Pickings? Auditioning for your own column in the Examiner?

OK. I'm sorry! Out of order! Let's start again.

But, to be fair, as you'll hear, this thing with Char *is* almost becoming a soap, Leicester's very own version of EastEnders or Corrie. I've just got to remember what's happening is horrible and sad. And real. It's all too easy to start getting cheap thrills out of other people's misfortune, isn't it?

So, as unsensationally as possible…

Pete had been watching the rugby on Sky during Sunday afternoon, 'reading' the *News on Sunday* (not!), and later in the evening when I flopped down in front of the telly, I picked the paper up and started flicking through it mindlessly. I think they must coat these Sunday rags with magic dust. You find yourself powerless to resist, drawn to the yuckiness. Well, I do, anyway! Funnily enough, I'd been thinking about Char just beforehand, wondering what to do about the fact she hadn't called me since Friday night. (Am I being silly? It just felt wrong for me to be the one picking up the phone!)

Anyway, somewhere in the middle, my eye caught a story headlined *Mistress of Foxhounds*. Now I'm not a 'meat is murder' type, but if there's one thing which gets me going, it's grown people chasing terrified little foxes about for sport. Why not shoot them, if there are too many? So I suppose that's what got me hooked. But of course, it wasn't about fox-hunting at all, it was about some posh Master of Foxhounds who'd been having an affair. The details were all very sordid. What they did and where they did it. Too much information! But it wasn't like he was the Prime Minister or anyone, so who should care?

The details of the people didn't mean anything to me at first. And then I looked at the photo. It was Mrs Ellison. Not the slightest doubt about it, despite the dark glasses and the headscarf. And yes, further down there was her name – Samantha Ellison.

I sat there for a few moments, fascinated enough to reread the article on the one hand, and on the other, disgusted enough to want to tear it up and throw it in the bin. Then, as a compromise, I took the *News on Sunday* out of the sitting room and stuffed it in the middle of a pile of magazines under my bed, so no other Goodenough would see the offending piece and put two and two together. Because I'd already started to assume, though of course I may have been completely wrong, that this stuff about her mum might have had a lot to do with Char getting off her head on Friday.

OK. So what on earth was I going to say to Char the next morning now? As I banged my head on my pillow before I went to sleep (seven times to make sure I woke at seven o'clock – try it, and see if it works for you!), I figured I'd have to wing it.

I was pretty wired when I hit Willowmede on Monday. When Em remarked to me before school, quite innocently, 'I haven't seen Char today. Do you know where she is?' I snapped her head off.

'No,' I said, 'why do you want to know?'

'Wow. Who rattled your cage, superstar?' she retorted. 'School too boring for you these days?'

Why do we so get it wrong with each other at the moment?

In fact, Char didn't show all day, and there wasn't a phone call during Monday evening either. I sent a *How R U?* text as soon as I got home but there wasn't a reply to that, and I kept playing with the buttons on my mobile, wondering whether to try to talk to her properly. I didn't. Maybe she needed the space.

69

However, on Tuesday morning there was a card in the post, a very nice card with a picture of a garden overflowing with large green leaves in every imaginable shade, and a cat hiding among them. Inside, it simply said, 'Thank you!' with Char's big, careful signature and a kiss. And at the bottom was written, 'Cat = Me! Might be out of school for a few days. No probs! Everything's OK.' Who did she think she was kidding?

Char's private life hasn't been the only weird vibe at Willowmede this week. Eddie Finn has started following me around. At first, I thought I was imagining it when I kept tripping over him by my locker or at the school gate, but it's been happening too often for coincidence. Mostly he's just mumbled, 'How ya doing?', before pretending to be on his sluggy way somewhere else. Sometimes, he hasn't even got as far as talking. Instead there's been a strange non-verbal hello, a twitchy nod of the head ending up midway between a leer and a wink. All very odd. The most bizarre moment came on Thursday afternoon when he started walking along with me in the direction of home. You've got to imagine the long trademark pauses before Eddie says the next thing on his mind. Maybe his brain works very slowly or he needed to find fresh courage for each line.

'Is Drew, like, your boyfriend, then?' he began, after about two hundred metres of silent companionship.

'No!' I said, giving him my best withering look and lengthening my stride purposefully.

Pause.

' 'Cos... 'Cos you two seem to hang out together a lot...'

'I hang out a lot with other people too. You at the moment.'

Maybe that was the wrong thing to say.

Pause.

'Girls and that...'

'Well, yeah, but so what?'

Long pause.

'Well, he's, like, a boy...'

I could have gone very sarcastic on him, e.g. 'You've noticed! Good at Biology, are you?' I restrained myself. Just.

'I've known Drew since I was four, Eddie. I can't remember ever *not* being mates with Drew.'

Exceptionally long pause.

'So he's not your boyfriend then?'

I got the drift. Things were going to get increasingly embarassing from here, so I jumped in fast.

'I don't think I'd know where to fit in having a boyfriend,' I said, sounding relentlessly upbeat. 'Anyway, it's fab being part of a crowd. Wasn't it great when we all went out together last week?'

Pause.

'Yeah,' he said, with all the enthusiasm of someone who was about to have a bucket of dung emptied over his head. 'Yeah. S'pose so! See ya, then!' And he veered off miserably down a convenient side street, tail apparently between his legs. Tough!

Or should that be 'Poor Eddie'? I don't know! But I *do* know I'm not the answer to any of his prayers or problems.

Last lesson on a Tuesday is French with Penny. This week, there we were in the middle of *La vie en supermarché*, trying to learn how to complain if we were ever in a supermarket in Marseilles or Montmartre and the meat was off, when there was a knock on the door, and Zoe Hughes appeared.

'Sorry to bother you, Mr Farthing,' she said sweetly, 'but could we borrow Abi for a few moments?'

If you're me, your guilty conscience always makes you wonder what you've done at such moments, and of course, I instantly thought of Char.

'If you promise faithfully to bring her back,' said Penny heavily. 'There'll be a fine for her late return!'

By his standards, that has to be counted as clutch-your-stomach humour.

'Any problem, Miss Hughes?' I said nervously, when we were in the corridor.

She read my mind and laughed, before she bounced away on some other errand. 'No need to worry, Abi,' she said. 'Dr Dickson just wanted to have a word. Something nice, I think!'

AD has his own minuscule room where he supplies tissues for the bullied and broken-hearted and applies thumbscrews to scallies. It's hard to get three people in there, but just about possible if you're prepared to touch knees. Today the third person apart from him and me was Rosie Pickings. Interesting! Perhaps Zoe Hughes wanted me there as a chaperone. Given the length of Rosie Pickings' skirt (thigh-high and worn without tights), I wouldn't have been surprised. Good grief, now I'm sounding like Gran! They shuffled chairs and we got cosy.

'You remember Miss Pickings, don't you?' AD began.

My mind was racing, trying to work out the angles here, given a) my opinion on her article about Willowmede, b) my opinion of newspapers in general after the Samantha Ellison thing and c) not having a clue about any of AD's current opinions about Rosie or any of these matters.

'Yes, hello!' I said politely in what Em would have probably called my 'head-girl voice'.

'Well now, Abi,' smirked AD, 'Miss Pickings…'

'Please call me Rosie…'

Watch out Hughesey! She's after your man!

'*Rosie*… is going to spend the day in school tomorrow, because she wants to write another article about Willowmede.' He looked at the *Examiner*'s Education Reporter questioningly. 'Isn't that right?'

'A day in the life of an academy,' Rosie confirmed, beaming broadly and crossing her legs. More thigh was on show than seemed decently possible. The room temperature rose a few more degrees.

'And what I'd like,' AD went on, trying very hard to concentrate, but not on Rosie's legs, 'is for you to look after her during the day.'

He handed me a sheet of printed A4.

'So here's a programme of events, which includes a number of your lessons, Abi. I'd like you to collect Rosie when the schedule says, and show her around as I've indicated. The rest of the time you can take as private study. Then, if she's not totally exhausted [*little playful laugh*. Yuk!], she can come to the A Club session on 'Study Skills' after school. Is that OK with you, Rosie? Does that give you what you need?'

'Excellent,' she breathed.

'Happy with that Abi? All clear?'

I nodded, still trying to get a grip. A whole day. Being nice to Rosie Pickings. Now that was a challenge!

While we were dancing around each other to say goodbye, trying not to tread on each other's toes or touch inappropriately, there was a knock at the door, and Zoe Hughes materialized again, looking puzzled. 'I'm sorry to interrupt, Dr Dickson,' she said, 'but Mr Soteriou's here to see us?'

AD's worry lines appeared. 'He's not supposed to be here until tomorrow,' he said. 'Is he?'

'That's what *I* thought,' said Hughesey, with a nervous giggle.

Then the penny dropped. Mr Soteriou was the expert on study skills, and get this, *time management*, due to take the session with the A Club the following day. An expert on time management who couldn't keep a diary properly! Nice one! I imagined Rosie Pickings sharpening her pencil already. But she was fiddling inside her handbag, and seemed oblivious to any cock-ups on the management front.

AD's notes said I had to meet Rosie at the school office at ten to nine on Wednesday, and take her to the year assembly, where she was to have the big thrill of seeing AD strut his I-am-dictator-of-the-Western-world-well-at-least-Year-Nine stuff. I thought I was being clever by being five minutes early. But so was Rosie. I offered her my hand, which she probably wasn't expecting. Her grip was limp and feeble. Dad says you can tell a lot about someone from their handshake.

Wednesday was apparently Rosie's dress-down day. Today there wasn't anything to frighten the horses or excite the Year Eleven boys: black trousers, blue silk shirt (with just the one button undone), black cardigan and sensible shoes. Subtle traces of unidentified flowery perfume. At first glance, she could have been a new Geography teacher. But it did strike me as a bit weird that she managed to look so very different to the previous day. Different hair (highlights today), different make-up (no red eyeshadow). Even the shape of her face seemed to have changed. Very clever. Welcome, Rosie Pickings: Mistress of Disguise! Maybe the previous day we'd caught her on the back of interviewing Billie Piper or Jordan.

Apart from the wet fish handshake, OK, she was as friendly as ever, big eyes and a warm smile. If it wasn't for the fact I don't trust her further than I can spit, there are lots of reasons to like Rosie Pickings. She could even be one of Deb's mates, the way she puts herself about.

Rosie showed no signs of wanting to hurry down to the hall for AD's morning Sieg Heil.

'What does the idea of an Academy mean to you, Abi?' she asked. I gulped and tried to focus.

'I think it's like, they want to make things better for us... You know, so more people do well in exams and stuff?'

Not exactly a sound bite, but I thought if I got quoted, at least it couldn't cause any trouble.

'Will it work, then?' she asked, smiling encouragingly.

I couldn't make out whether she genuinely wanted to know, or if this was an invitation to put my foot in it. I decided to play safe.

'I don't know,' I said. 'I should think it's a bit early to tell, don't you? I know they're spending a lot of money. [*Lots of enthusiasm!*] We can go and look at the building site later if you want?'

She looked at me hard.

'Yes,' she said, 'I gather you're having to do some of your lessons down the road at Brooklands. That must be very disruptive?'

'Same teachers,' I said. 'Just a different place. And it'll be nice when the whole of Willowmede's as brilliant as the theatre, won't it?'

'Yes,' she said, uncertainly. I think Rosie didn't quite know what to make of me and my diplomacy. Was she hoping I'd dish the dirt, if she caught me before I'd woken up? 'Right, we'd better show our faces at this assembly then, hadn't we?'

Mentally I scored myself a little tick. First round to Abi.

Year Nine assemblies are pretty tame affairs. You do hear rumours of things getting out of hand in Years Ten and Eleven: teachers getting booed, year heads losing it, mass walkouts, stuff like that, but AD's pretty much got it down, so I suppose from Big Ben's point of view, assembly was a low-risk activity for visitors with attitude.

Sylvester's class was giving a presentation on the famine in Africa. They'd borrowed some of those awful images of starving kids with flies covering their faces, and behind the pictures they played haunting, sad African music. Over the music, Syl read out the stats of the numbers of children who are dying every day from hunger and disease. You'd have had to be a complete no-brain not to be moved. The hall went pin-drop quiet. Yeah, OK, I wept a quiet tear or two. I wiped them quickly away from my cheek with a sleeve and shot a quick look at Rosie. Her face was a mask. If she was feeling anything, you'd not have known. Is that what it takes to be a journalist, then?

After assembly, Rosie came with me to a Maths class, which I'd have thought would have bored the pants off her. But she smiled for Britain the whole way through it, occasionally jotting things down on an electronic notepad. Perhaps Maths had always been her favourite subject. Maybe something had gone out of her life when she'd closed the textbook that last time.

Afterwards, I walked her down the road to Brooklands, and English with Sandy Johnson. At the moment, Sandy's into conflict and tribes, and how a bit of a rumble often makes for a good book or play, particularly if there's a family feud somewhere in the plot. If that's true, maybe I could sell an autobiography of the Goodenoughs. There's that book about gangs in the East End of London, which is a yawn only 'cos we first read it in Year Six and everyone knows it off by heart, and *Romeo and Juliet* of course, and we've spent a couple of double periods watching the film of *West Side Story* (which I seem to be the only one to find amazingly fab).

So, on Wednesday, with a young woman to impress, he decides we're going to pull back the chairs and tables and do an impro show. And naturally, Sandy's got to be right in there too. He's the self-appointed cheerleader for one of the two sides in this football aggro story he's invented. Reds vs Whites.

Everyone gets a card with instructions written on them as to who they are and what they're supposed to think and do. We're going to build up the drama, he says, and then write about it.

'Would you like to join in?' Sandy shouts through the rising chaos at Rosie, who'd clearly like to be somewhere else at this moment. 'Or are you happier just watching?'

She makes a gesture with her hands as if to say, 'It's fine. You just start without me!', and while the rest of us throw ourselves into murder and mayhem on the streets of imaginary Mudchester, Rosie shrinks further and further into her corner of the room. And I'm thinking, *So why did Big Ben and AD imagine this was such a good idea?*

The thing is, the whole world likes Sandy, and actually us kids know we've only got just so much rope, so although his lessons can sometimes look like World War Three's broken out, really it's slightly more controlled than that.

Only this time, there's a hitch. The large book cupboard in the Brooklands classroom has become an alleyway in the drama, and at some point the cupboard door (accidentally?) closes on the two kids and Sandy who are inside it, supposedly hiding from the gang which is chasing them, and then the handle comes off the *outside* of the door and for some reason Sandy and co. seem unable to open it from the *inside*. Of course, everyone in the class finds this extremely falling-about amusing, and no one apart from Sandy is in much of a hurry to sort the door out. Rosie looks terrified, wondering if as the only other adult she should take charge, throwing nervous glances this way and that. Maybe she should call the caretaker or Big Ben? Or the cops!

Then, all of a sudden, we hear Sandy putting his full shoulder weight on the door, there's the sound of wood splitting, the door gives way, and he emerges, falling forward, sprawling full length on the floor, looking convincingly like he really has just been coshed by some crazed footie supporter. And from the corner of my eye through the classroom's glass windows, I see Big Ben padding the corridor on his hush puppies, having walked all the way down from the main campus just to see how Rosie's enjoying her day. He spots the scenes of carnage inside, and then softly tiptoes backwards out of sight. Better not to interfere with Mr Johnson's lesson. Such a creative teacher!

I'm not the only one to see Big Ben. While Sandy's taking a few seconds to work out if he's concussed, Rosie stands and gives BB a little half wave, all in vain. Stephen Thompson, who'll dance on anyone's grave, shouts out, 'Ooh, sir. There's Mr Browning, sir. Do you think you'll get into trouble, sir? For breaking the cupboard door?' Because, it's true, the door *is* now resting on its hinges at an interesting and unintended angle.

Order is finally restored amid much hilarity. Towards the end of the lesson, we actually do some writing, but afterwards Rosie, who looks a bit paler now than she did, asks me, 'Are all Mr Johnson's lessons like that?'

I sidestep the question. 'I really want to do GCSE Drama,' I say. 'All Mr Johnson's pupils get As and A*s!'

I don't know if this is a complete porky, but I reckon Sandy deserves the break.

At break, I took Rosie back to the main campus staff room, and then handed her over to watch some Year Eleven Science lessons, while I went to the library. After a while, AD loomed over my shoulder. I don't know what he'd heard about Rosie's exposure to live theatre but, 'Everything going well, Abi?' he asked, a bit doubtfully.

'Think so, sir,' I lied.

People, I mean, *adult* people, forget, you know. They forget that school is really hard work. No strolling off to the coffee machine when we feel like it. No games of patience or golf on our workstations. No payslip to look forward to. No perks. We just have our noses rubbed on the grindstone every day, all day. Rosie came out of Science looking completely bushed.

'OK?' I asked.

'Smelly,' she said, and laughed wearily. 'Brought back memories. Not necessarily good ones!'

Em passed us in the lunch hall as I was about to park Rosie at a table.

'Grovel, grovel! Creep, creep! Head Girl!' she hissed.

'Come and join us, Em,' I said loudly, 'why don't you?'

The schedule had said it would be nice if Rosie got to share her lunch with a cross section of Willowmede students.

Em pulled a face, but sat down anyway. Soon she was gabbling to Rosie like she'd known her all her life. Sally Kennedy arrived with a buddy of hers, and then Eddie Finn was suddenly there, sitting next to me (bother!) and pushing his way into Em's conversation.

'Nice motor you've got,' he said to Rosie.

'Thank you,' said Rosie.

'Saw you parking it this morning,' Eddie continued. 'Lovely machines, those little Mazdas...'

And off they went about overhead camshafts etc etc. To her credit, Rosie gave as good as she got.

'How fast does it go?' went Eddie.

'How would I know that? You don't think I'd break the speed limit, do you now?'

'Go on with you!'

Eddie was flirting! Good grief! He must have a thing for older women too.

'Well, OK. I do know ninety-five's no problem...'

'And probably no more than three and a half thou on the rev counter, I bet!'

And so on and so on. After another ten minutes of automotive engineering, when they'd just got on to aerodynamics, Em couldn't hold it any longer and had a fit of the giggles.

'Don't mind her,' I said. 'She often gets like that. Rosie, it's 12.45.

Time for the building site?'

'Do I have to?' she said. 'I'd much rather stay here with you guys and natter.'

It was a nice thing to say, but it was just schmooze.

At that moment, Miss Everard walked by. She caught sight of Rosie and suddenly seemed fascinated by what she saw. *Rude woman*, I thought, *Hasn't anyone told you, you shouldn't stare?* I thought for a moment she was going to interrupt us, but then she changed her mind and moved on. Had they met before? I suppose it's possible.

The idea was to deliver Rosie to the site entrance where she was to meet Big Ben and one of the contractors, put on a hard hat, and inspect the foundations of the new sports hall. Personally, I'd have thought that would be dead boring, but seeing she was so much into overhead camshafts, maybe not. When we got there, Big Ben was looking dead embarassed, the contractor was arguing with the foreman, and a few of the builders were throwing spades and hats into a barrow, like they were packing up early for the day.

'Um, a bit of a, um, minor industrial dispute, Miss Pickings,' said Big Ben from some feet above my head. How tall is he? Six foot ten? Leiccster's lighthouse, I once heard someone call him. 'Would you, um, perhaps like to come up to my room for a coffee and a chat? I'm sure it'll all be smoothed over shortly.'

'That's what you think, sunshine!' said a very Irish voice, just loud enough to hear.

After her interview with BB, Rosie obviously had a whale of a time at our mid-afternoon art class. So she should have! The Art rooms at Willowmede are like Aladdin's Cave. Some of the stuff the A level students do is flabbergasting. I can't imagine being that good in four years' time. Then Rosie took herself off to hear a lecture the Year Twelves were having on HIV/AIDS.

'It's OK. I'll find my way,' she said confidently.

'Sure?'

'No probs. I'm good at remembering places,' she said, laughing a funny little laugh. Just then, I had the feeling there was something

I didn't understand.

After school at a quarter past four, there were six of us A Clubbers in the library plus Rosie, Hughesey and AD, but no Mr Soteriou. AD looked as if he might commit murder.

'I'll just give him a call,' he said through clenched teeth, and left the room. When he came back, he said (mostly to Rosie!), 'I am so sorry, everyone! Apparently Mr Soteriou is unwell. And his wife forgot to phone and tell us.'

Having heard the previous day's conversation, this struck me as incredibly funny, but AD obviously wasn't seeing it the same way.

'It's all right,' said Zoe Hughes. 'Who needs Mr Soteriou? Find me some pencils and a box of scrap paper, Dr Dickson.'

And for the next forty-five minutes, Hughesey did just the best and most entertaining session on study skills. What a brilliant teacher she is!

Drew lapped it up. 'This is fantastic,' he said to me at one point. AD was like he'd been saved from the guillotine. And the way he looked at Hughesey, you could tell it was love.

But then, right at the end of the day, Willowmede managed to snatch defeat from the jaws of victory. As we went out into the late afternoon sunshine to escort Rosie to her Mazda, and allow Eddie one last coo over automobile perfection, the sound of rhythmic, male war-chanting floated across on the breeze from the corner of the car park. Just by the exit to the road, a circle of Year Ten and Eleven boys in Willowmede sweatshirts was surrounding a pair of kids who, with eyes blazing, were grappling on the ground, throwing punches indiscriminately at each other's body and face. One of the boys was a Willowmede pupil: the other was clearly in Ratcliffe School colours.

AD's face went white with anger as he moved in to pull them apart.

'Nothing much changes then, does it?' remarked Rosie drily.

Well, it's Sunday lunchtime and still there hasn't been a reply from

Char. I've tried ringing her mobile repeatedly but a silly voice keeps telling me her number isn't available at present, and though I've left messages, she hasn't answered any of them. I prayed hard about her in church this morning. So all I can do is hope God's looking after her, whatever's going down.

Blog the Seventh
23 October

Typical Pete. You'd have thought I could rely on him to leave his *News on Sunday* lying around the one week I needed it. I was desperate to know what was going on with Char and her family. But, of course, relying on Pete isn't much of a life plan. For once on a Sunday afternoon, the sitting room was just the way Mum likes it: not an ornament out of place, and not a crumb let alone a paper spoiling the dizzying pattern of the carpet. I couldn't very well ask Pete where he'd stashed the *NOS* without damaging my family rep, so late in the afternoon I pretended to be in urgent need of choccy, and jogged up to the petrol station which, like they do, seems more interested in selling you newspapers, chocolate and cuddly toys than petrol. I bought a couple of hits of Cadbury's finest and then, like it was an afterthought, the offending article.

Back home, I made a big deal out of scoffing the chocolate and smuggled the paper up to my room underneath my anorak.

From my research over the years (do you read the *Sun*? Do you read *Heat*? No, but it's hard to avoid other people's! At school. On the buses), I've got the hang that they like to run these kind of shock horror stories for more than just a single week. As I'd guessed, in the middle of this week's *NOS* was a page dedicated to keeping the nation in the loop about the crucially important events in Thornton Bramleigh.

They'd printed another picture of Samantha Ellison, this time looking far more relaxed and glam than the previous week. It described her as an 'elegant former model' and the headline ran, 'We didn't want to hurt anyone'. A bit late for that, Samantha.

Char's mum had given them an interview. She didn't come out of it very well, because she pretty much blamed everyone from primary school upwards for taking advantage of her. Particularly, of course, the Master of Foxhounds. The paper described gleefully how he'd been kicked out of his job last week (serves him right too!). Mrs E was quoted as saying she hoped her family could be reunited despite the affair 'for the sake of my daughter'. At least the paper had the decency not to mention Char's name.

I kept my mobile switched on and beside me all evening. For some reason I had a premonition Char would finally call, and she did too, at about nine o'clock, just when I was about to give up, have a bath and go to bed.

'Hi, it's me. Char!' she croaked.

'Hello stranger,' I answered cheerily. 'How's the cat?'

She didn't get it for a moment.

'The card?' I prompted her.

'Oh right...' she said. Char's voice was lifeless, drained of every ounce of energy. 'Not so good. Not really. There's been a bit of a problem. At home...' she added, so quietly I could scarcely hear her.

'Yes, I know.'

'You know? Oh, God!'

'It's OK. I just happened to see Pete's paper. It was in there. I could easily have missed it...'

Liar!

'Have you said anything to anyone?'

'No, of course not. And no one's said anything to me. But why didn't you call me?' I was trying not to sound like I was blaming her. Unsuccessfully, I think.

'Mum took my mobile away,' she said.

'She did what? That's outrageous!'

'No, no... Listen, it was sensible really. The press were doorstepping the house. We didn't know who they might use to get to us. So Mum just made sure she could shut things down for the week. Till she'd talked to them properly – told her side of the story! Did you see that too?'

'Yeah.'

There was a long silence at the other end.

'You still there, Char?' I asked. 'Tell me. What happens now?'

'Dad's left.' Char's voice was the merest whisper.

'Do you think he'll come back?' I asked softly.

'Don't know. Shouldn't think so. Would *you* come back?'

There was another long pause. 'Mum keeps talking about wanting to get away,' she continued eventually. 'Don't know where that leaves me…'

'You going to be in school this week?'

'S'pose so. Rather be there than anywhere else.'

'Well, I'm sure the offer still stands,' I said. 'Come and stay at our place for a few days. If you want…'

She almost bit my hand off this time. 'Could I? Really?'

'You can have my bed if necessary. I'll sleep on the floor.'

'Let me work on Mum,' Char said, sounding slightly re-energized. 'She might need some convincing, even though she says she wants to get away…'

I rang off reluctantly, leaving Char to cope with whatever in Thornton Bramleigh. A chorus of police sirens nee-nawed their way mournfully along the dual carriageway at the end of our road.

'Just listen to that!' Dad harrumphed, as I went past him up the stairs to run my bath. 'What is it this time, I wonder?'

'PC Plod late for a hot date,' I joked.

Wrong! As I found out when we pitched up at Willowmede on Monday morning. Four police cars were parked up on the verges at the school entrance, 4x4s, parents and kids were churning about, and a large, hastily written sign said all Year Sevens, Eights and Nines should go immediately to the theatre on arrival. Inside there was pandemonium. The swipe card security system had broken down for the umpteenth time, and the foyer was churning with kids yapping and larking about. Anarchy in the UK.

The goss was that some toerags, ages and backgrounds unknown, had broken in on Sunday evening, pinched as many computers as they could and tried to torch a wing of the main block. The fire brigade had arrived in time to stop the fire spreading, but there was enough smoke and water damage for the school to want to get shot of all the lower years for a couple of days while Big Ben and his sidekicks thought about what to do. Apparently it had been headline news on *Motorway FM*'s local radio drivetime show. Not much good to me, amongst others. It's Strictly Come Radio 4 in our house.

In the theatre, a stressed-out AD separated truth from fiction (Big Ben had *not* topped himself, and *no* members of staff were helping the police with their enquiries) and told everyone to push off home unless there was no one at home to push off to, in which case they should let him know. Then he asked various people to see him. Included were the A Clubbers, so I guessed we were about to be dumped on. Next event in the A Club diary was a talk to be given in the theatre on Thursday by Dame Jessica Taft. It was a fair bet arrangements for the lecture were going pear-shaped.

The A Club Seven assembled by the stage in the middle of a crowd of teachers and pupils. No one was sure whether to look gutted or shout hallelujah.

'Hi Char!' shouted Em over the racket. 'You feeling better this week?'

'What?' Char replied. 'Oh yeah. Yeah! Heaps better. Doctor said it was a virus...' Too quick. Too offhand. I wouldn't have believed her for a minute.

AD corralled us to one side where we could just about hear his voice above the din. 'It 's an ill wind,' said AD, rubbing his forehead and smoothing back his hair. He looked very grey and seedy and un-AD-like. 'Difficult day. *Really* difficult day! Look, I could do with your help, guys...'

The 'guys' thing was a dead giveaway. I was right. There'd been a foul-up with the Jessica Taft thing. Of course there had. A pattern is emerging. A Club event = impending disaster!

Who is Jessica Taft, you ask? Well, apparently she's an ace yachtswoman who sailed single-handed round the world with her hands tied behind her back. Or something like that. And years ago she was an ace ballerina with the Royal Ballet too. For that reason, I'd been quite looking forward to hearing her talk, except it meant

I'd miss Tomorrow's People again and Jana would go mental.

'Well, despite last night's events, we'll still go ahead with Thursday, come hell or high water,' said AD. Rather fittingly, I thought. 'But... er... thing is... there've been a few problems with publicity.' He rubbed his forehead again. He looked short of sleep.

'Look, a few weeks ago we got the local Rotary Club involved...' (What's a Rotary Club? Sounds like a bunch of people going round in circles.) '... because Mr Browning's their president this year...' (*Ah, another bunch of do-gooders!*) '... and they've already got the local sailing clubs circulated, but I'd promised we'd do our bit in spreading the word. However, I'm afraid with all the hoo-hah, I just haven't got round to it...'

But the hoo-hah's only 24 hours old, AD! So what's with the excuses? Never mind, we'll bail you out, won't we? Bail? Boats? Jessica Taft? Get it? Ha ha!

'Char and Abi, I'd like *you* to go along to *Motorway FM* at eleven o'clock? Ask for Jeremy Battison. He's going to interview you about Jessica Taft. He'll be expecting you. I was going to do it, but with all this...'

AD spread his arms in a gesture of despair and shoved a load of stuff about sailing at Char – Jessica Taft's book and some handouts.

'This tells you everything you need to know. If you go downtown now, you'll be in plenty of time to mug up before the radio show. And make sure you say A Club and Willowmede a lot. OK? And the rest of you... Look, I'm really sorry to ask this... but could you spend a couple of hours this morning trying to get these flyers into as many shops and public places as you can?'

I could see from the set of her jaw that Em was stropping up, and I didn't blame her. This division of labour might solve AD's problem but it smacked of 'teacher's pets'. Em and the others got to do the hard graft, while Char and I swanned off to be guest celebrities on *Motorway FM*. Bad choice, AD, though he wasn't to know that.

'Sir,' I said, 'why not let Em or one of the others do the radio thing instead of me?'

Very noble. Very diplomatic. Or so I thought.

But, uncharacteristically, AD went all snappy on me. Whatever you say about the bloke in terms general oiliness, at least he's usually pretty relaxed. Clearly this morning had really got to him.

'Look, Abi,' he said, 'don't argue, OK? Just do as I ask! Please!'

Em looked poisonously at him. And me.

We traipsed out towards the gates, amid the general hubbub. There were still various conspiracy theories doing the rounds. One even had Big Ben down as the master criminal, twisting Logic Solutions' arm for bigger and newer computers.

Who should be coming in as we were going out but Rosie Pickings. She seemed to have regenerated overnight as Punk Girrl, all purple lipgloss, gelled-up hair and leather trousers. Maybe it's her regular crime reporter's outfit.

Char and I happened to be two steps in front of the others.

'Hi guys,' Rosie said to us. 'Extra day off, eh?' Then (and the question sounded perfectly innocent), 'Sorry, Abi, I don't know your friend's name...'

Like an utter muppet, I opened my mouth without thinking and answered, 'It's Char... Charlotte Ellison.' And then a millisecond later realized what I'd done.

There was a barely perceptible movement in Rosie's eyes, and my heart sank into my boots. I knew at once she'd made the connection. Her brain was already calculating how many Ellisons there were in the phone book, and the chances of *this* Ellison being a significant one.

'You A Clubbers are quite a bunch, aren't you?' she said slyly. 'What with Bobby Kennedy's daughter and all of that? It's just so hard to keep you out of the limelight.'

The whole conversation passed so quickly, I wasn't even sure Char had clocked it, but to me, still jangled up from being steamrollered by AD, it rang the loudest alarm bells. And just what had Rosie written about Willowmede after her visit last week? We wouldn't find out until lunchtime.

As we went out of the gates, Em was still chuntering behind me about the unfairness of life and teachers, so I turned round and said as pleasantly as I could, 'Look, just give us half your flyers. It's no big deal. Tell us where you're going, and Char and I'll find somewhere else in town to do our share!'

'Wouldn't dream of it,' she answered airily. 'You go off and have your fun! Anyway, who'd want to do that radio thing? Have you *heard* Jeremy Battison? He's a complete bimbo!'

Give me a break, Em!

But of course, though I felt dead guilty the whole way through, the radio thing *was* fun, and Jeremy Battison was very nice and un-bimbo-like, despite his dodgy permed hair. I don't *think* we were airheads, but on the other hand I'm glad no one (Mum, for instance) knew we were going to be on, so I didn't have to listen back later to what we said.

Thereafter Char and me spent a fairly fruitless hour trying to persuade people to put up our posters, before giving up and heading for Café Doppio. We sat in the café window and watched the world go by, and I tried to mix mindless goss with letting Char be gloomy. Then, blow me, after about half an hour, Em suddenly strolled past with Sally Kennedy. Sal spotted us and waved. Em scowled. I smiled enthusiastically and beckoned them to come and join us, but Em shook her head, hunched her shoulders and walked on. Sally shrugged and followed.

'What would you do with it?' I sighed at Char, but her mind was miles away in Thornton Bramleigh, and she wasn't interested in Em's spat with me.

We bought an *Examiner* and opened it up, fearing the worst. But there was nothing to worry about there. Rosie's article about Willowmede as an academy was very low-key. No scandal, no big deal about the things that had gone wrong during the previous Wednesday, not even a mention of the scrap in the car park.

'Well, I still don't trust her,' Char said morosely.

'Me neither,' I agreed. Char had little reason to trust anyone right now. I just hoped to goodness I hadn't increased the risk to Char from Rosie by my carelessness.

When I finally got home on Monday afternoon, I threw my bag down with a sigh of relief. Thanks to the school break-in I still had one whole, long, unexpected day to do what I liked with. At the Monday tap class, I arranged with Ciarán to go in and use Tuesday afternoon to do some extra work on my dance pieces for the festival.

'About time,' she said ungraciously. 'You're not in any sort of shape to perform!'

Gee, thanks, Ciarán!

I phoned Jana and arranged to see her at teatime.

'Thought you'd gone off to be a missionary,' was *her* witty one-liner.

Excellent!

These adults really do think we exist just in their own little universe, for their benefit and exclusive use. We disappear when we're not with them. We have no other life.

When Mum came in, I told her what had happened at school, and mentioned the possibility of Char's spending a few days with us.

'Good!' she said, triumphantly. 'Your room's a disgrace! I don't know how you can live like that. And we certainly can't have Char thinking we live like pigs. You can use tomorrow morning to tidy up!'

That bit about pigs. A slight exaggeration, I think! The usual homework scatter, some minor clothing chaos, a bit of fluff here and there. Nothing more.

Halfway through the evening, during *Chavs and Boffs*, TV's latest, and possibly most-mindless-to-date reality show (you know what it's going to be about, don't you, without me telling you!), someone sounding faintly like my old friend Em called on the mobile. But this person was sulky, narky and self-obsessed.

'Coming shopping tomorrow?' No preliminaries to the demand.

My instinct was to say yes, anything, just so long as we can be mates. But by then I'd realized tomorrow wasn't possible, not if I was going to write up Sandy Johnson's football piece, and dance at Ciarán's *and* waft my fiddle around for an hour. And if I didn't do *that*, there was every chance of looking a complete prat at the festival.

'Oh, I'm sorry Em, I can't!'

'What do you mean, you can't?'

'I'm *really* sorry, Em. I've got too much on.'

'Like what?'

I was a bit peeved at her tone, so I ran the long list of things to do past her. I was probably beginning to sound a tad stroppy myself.

'OK. Whatever!' she said belligerently.

I checked the temptation to yell.

'Look, what about Saturday?' I pleaded desperately. 'Let's go to the cinema…'

Em made as if this was the most boring idea ever devised, but after various sucking-teeth and humming and ha-ing noises, said half-heartedly, 'Oh, all right, then!' like I had her in an armlock.

On Wednesday, I practically crawled back into school on my knees. What is it with all these moaning, ungrateful people? I shall name and shame them.

Mum and I had half an hour's 'quality time' together over Tuesday breakfast before she went to her committee meeting. What did she use it for? To complain that she never saw me during the week and was sure I wasn't getting enough schoolwork done.

Ciarán ran me ragged all Tuesday afternoon. Apparently I'm not strong enough, not disciplined enough and have no sense of rhythm or line. Oh, and when I perform I don't smile the way I used to. Hello? Just give me something to smile about, Ciarán!

Jana made me feel guilty for an hour, because apparently everyone looks up to me, she says, and when I'm not there, Tomorrow's People doesn't work properly. Well, yes, I'm a year older than the rest of them and it's true. They sometimes act like a herd of brainless drongoes if I'm not around to say provoking things like, 'How can you prove God exists?' or 'Is it *always* wrong to have sex before you marry?' But why do I have to be the sheepdog who keeps the herd together all the time?

Then Drew was on the phone for an hour while I was trying to write *my* English homework, worrying that, despite all these new study skills he's working on – speed reading, keeping a diary, making notes, etc etc – none of it's any help when it comes down to knowing whether what he's writing for Sandy Johnson is crap or not.

'Drew,' I said eventually, practically tearing my hair out. 'You've just got to go for it. If *you* like what you're writing, isn't that good enough? Just do the best you can. It sounds great to me, and much better than what I'm doing, so DON'T WORRY!'

And how daft is this, I spent so much time listening to Drew that I completely lost the thread of my own Sandy Johnson piece, and it's rubbish!

I'm not joking. I'm fed up with everyone in my life at the moment, and before I went to sleep on Tuesday night, I had a little cry. Who's there for me when I need them? That's what I want to know.

On the slightly plus side, the Jessica Taft event was OK. That's if I'm being generous. More like an OK-minus really. You'd expect a dame to be large, imposing and old with big hair and lots of jewellery. In fact, JT turned out to be no bigger than me, with a very short cropped barnet dyed a rich red colour. I'd guess she's about Mum's age. But though the slides of her sailing derring-do were fab, and it made me think I might like to try out a bit of life on the ocean blue, she wasn't a very good speaker. Her voice was so quiet you sometimes really couldn't hear what she said.

The weather had suddenly turned freezing cold on Wednesday night; so much so that there was ice on the pavements on Thursday morning, and at one point during the day the sky went so greeny-dark I thought it might snow. Naturally, the heating had chosen that moment to go on the blink (does nothing in Willowmede work any longer?), so it was keep-your-coats-on time for JT's audience. And there wasn't much body heat to share on account of there not being many of us: even most of the Rotary Club had, like Eddie Finn, found something better to do. So not exactly a classic evening in the theatre.

And why were we six remaining A Clubbers there? What was it supposed to do for us? I mean, OK, JT's a very successful woman and all that, and I suppose we should be inspired, but I don't think any of us were. Except maybe to find careers as weather forecasters or heating engineers.

AD still looked harassed. And Hughesey was nowhere to be seen. Maybe they'd had a row? Hope not. You don't often think of teachers as human, but the way they sometimes look at each other almost makes you think they could be.

But let's not get soft, Abi. My point is: the reason we A Clubbers were freezing our rowlocks off in the theatre on Thursday wasn't anything to do with our educashun. It was to make AD look good. Tell me I'm wrong!

Afterwards, as we shivered on the Willowmede drive, waiting for Mum to come and pick us up, I tried to gee up a whingeing Em about Saturday afternoon. (She wasn't too cross with me to turn down a Goodenough lift home!) I wanted to see *Road Rage* which is one of those daft-funny animations like *Toy Story*, only this time it's about cars in a showroom who take on lives of their own. They embark on a quest to find the antidote for a mystery virus which is causing drivers to behave maniacally. Sounded like fun! Em was letting on it was far too juvenile for her sophisticated tastes, and I was just winning her round, when Char bounced up and announced, with all the tact of an American armoured division, 'Mum says if it's OK with you, she'll bring me over on Saturday afternoon, and I can stay as long as you'll have me.'

Em looked thunderous, while I floundered around, murmuring weakly, 'What about the morning, Char? No, I know! How about the evening? That might be better for us, actually,' etc etc.

Em didn't talk to me on the way home. Negotiations with Char continued throughout Friday, and in the end we agreed she'd come on Saturday evening. But why is nothing ever easy?

What emerged after a giggle-free Saturday afternoon at the cinema (the film was in fact awful and should have been car-crushed at birth!) was just how paranoiacally, humungously jealous Em is right now. Her self-image is nowhere. She thinks I don't want to be her friend any more, because she's not as interesting as Char, and her parents don't have the money that Char's do. Oh, and that she's going to grow up to be some kind of seven foot tall freak and she'll never have a boyfriend, and... and...

And of course I can't explain to Em about Char's real situation, which Em wouldn't want to swap for her own in a million years.

All my friends are idiots, and only some of them have excuses.

I woke up with a start in the middle of Sunday night, convinced I could hear a burglar moving round downstairs. I suppose I've had burglars on the brain ever since the Willowmede break-in. There were mysterious, indistinct, little noises which might have been someone bumping gently into the furniture ten feet under my bed. I thought I heard a hesitant cough, then some more creaks, and an intermittent shuffling, like a very large mouse had moved in.

It was clear enough that I was immediately fully awake, though obviously not fully in my right mind. Otherwise I wouldn't have picked up a hockey stick and gone down in my pyjamas to confront said burglar, would I?

I padded along the landing. Pete's door was closed and so was Mum and Dad's. I could hear Dad snoring. So it wasn't any of them. And there was no one else it could be, was there? Debs and Hannah were probably still partying the night away somewhere in the centre of Leicester before returning to their flats with or without their boyfriends. Somehow, Char's presence in the house had completely slipped my mind.

I tiptoed down the stairs and saw the sitting room door ajar. The shuffling was louder now. There was no doubt: it was coming from inside the room. I pushed the door. It creaked loudly, and I froze as it swung fully open, expecting to see a man in a striped jumper with a bag of our swag on his back, realizing only then that this had been a very, very stupid thing for me to do. Too late!

But it wasn't a burglar. Instead I saw Char, standing by the window, chin up and gazing steadily out into our garden. A beam of moonlight caught her in profile. Char's face was an unworldly creamy-white, to match the cotton of her extra large, extra long, t-shirt. Along with the fact that the moonlight had turned her lips purple, she looked like a poster from a Hammer Horror film. All it needed was a few drops of blood and we had *The Curse of the Vampires*. Her mouth was slightly open. She was staring intently out into the night, as if she were watching an animal or something. Extremely spooky!

Trying to control the shake in my voice, I called her name softly, twice, but Char kept going with badger-watch. Suddenly, though this was a first for me, it registered that Char must be sleepwalking. Which was very nearly as scary as meeting a burglar!

Heart pounding, I went up to her and touched her shoulder. I almost expected her to be cold to the touch, as should properly be the case with one of the living dead. But, of course, Char's skin was as warm as yours or mine, and I found I could turn her round and guide her back to the door and up the stairs to Debs and Hannah's old room, where I *now* remembered we'd settled her in twenty-four hours earlier. Once she was standing beside the bed, Char simply climbed in, rolled over and appeared to fall asleep. Lucky old Char!

I covered her up, watched her for a little while, shivered, and then went back to bed myself. *I* didn't sleep more than five minutes for the rest of the night, but there wasn't a peep out of Char till I took her a cup of tea at half past eight.

The whole of the previous evening had been slightly weird. As you're going to hear, perhaps it had all been a mistake as far as Char was concerned. It had left me with issues too, but at least I wasn't sleepwalking. Well, I don't think so, but how would you know?

Every now and then, St Michael's has a groovier Sunday evening service with the idea that you can bring along people who don't usually go to church. Well, the fickle finger of fate pointed at this being one of those Sundays, so I'd thought, why not give it a go? There was going to be a young worship band from Birmingham with a kick-ass rep (as Pete would say), and Adam, our curate, who's reckoned to be a bit of a hunk by some, was going to give a talk. And I couldn't think of what to do with Char on a half-term Sunday evening.

At present, you could probably invite Char to invade Belgium and she'd agree: she hasn't the energy for ideas of her own. So when I suggested St Michael's, she was like, yeah, go for it.

It was only when we walked through the church doors, and I began to see things through Char's eyes, that I had one of those moments when you realize with a shock how different other people's lives are. I mean, I've gone to church all my life. I don't give a second thought to the way the building looks inside: the choir stalls, the altar, the font, all the peculiar furniture and clothes. Or the way the people are: all over you like a rash when you walk in, completely silent before the service begins, waving their arms in the air when there's a song they like or know well. But if you're Char, and the only time you see a church is on the telly in soaps and stuff (which isn't usually like any church I've ever been in), it probably seems utterly mad.

The band *was* good. There was some stuff to move around to before the worship proper began (St Michael's is a big place and it's easy to shift the chairs for the normal congregation), and later some good rocky hymns everybody knew and sang along with raucously. Char seemed OK, though perhaps a bit fazed by so many people being friendly/nosey. She didn't sing the hymns, though you couldn't blame her for that. Even if she *had* known the words, I don't think she's much of a singer anyway.

But I really began to sweat when Adam started talking – both for me and for Char. He was talking about Jesus' story of the pearl of great price, and how, if we were really the Christians we should be, we'd put God before everything else, and be prepared to give up everything, even the most important possession we owned, for Him. And that we'd never be really happy unless we did this. And I'm thinking, *Yeah, OK, Adam, but how does that fit with school, and getting good exam grades? And doing what Mum and Dad want? And my dance and music and becoming famous or rich? Help!* It felt like enormous pressure, it really did, like a cement mixer churning up my insides, because you could do all that stuff, and it still wasn't enough for God. I didn't dare look at Char, particularly when Adam got on to sin stopping us from seeing how valuable the pearl was. Because when people talk about sin it seems to me they usually mean sex, and maybe if you are an Ellison, that's a sensitive subject right now.

Afterwards, at home, over mugs of de-stressing cocoa, I said cautiously, 'What did you think of St Michael's, then?'

'It was OK!' she said, sort of approvingly. That surprised me!

'You didn't feel like they were beating you over the head?'

'Well, I didn't understand a lot of it...'

'What did you think of Adam?'

Char ignored the question. The Char of a few weeks ago would have been raving about how fit he was. But all she said, rather wistfully, was, 'Everyone seemed very happy. It must be nice to have something that makes you so certain about life, Abs. I wish I was like you... I can't imagine that...'

I felt like a complete fraud. Because what *I* was thinking was, *Why is everyone at St Michael's so different from me? Don't these people have any problems in their lives? Why are they sticking their heads in the sand?*

But I couldn't say that to Char, could I? It felt like letting the side down.

Mustn't give the wrong impression though. I'm not so down on the world this week. Actually, rereading last week's blog, I feel a *lot* better than I did then. For a minute I thought about rewriting it, I sounded so depressed. Not that people haven't been on my back this week, because they have, even though this was supposed to be a half-term week and therefore my holiday. A *holiday*! Remember that idea, anyone?

I suppose one difference is that the festival has gone better than I had any right to expect, and in between various episodes of *War of the Dance Schools*, people have said some nice things about me. To Ciarán. And to my face. Good grief! Am I that shallow a person? Yes! Yes, I am!

Apart from the fiddle and jazz dance on Tuesday morning, all the festival events I was involved in were clustered together on Thursday and Friday, which left me with a lot of time to entertain Char during the first half of the week. Not that she needed much entertaining, to be fair. If there was a spare moment on a bus, or while I was doing my festival thing or whatever, Char'd pull out a paperback, and instantly be lost in her book of the day. Dad's like that with his napping. He can fall asleep anywhere, at a moment's notice. Char seems to be into American cops and robbers at the moment. I picked one up. Grossly gruesome! Body parts and murder weapons.

Char also turns out to be a complete shopaholic, so now I understand much more than I want about the contents of Leicester's department stores. Cosmetics. Underwear. China. Furniture. It all seems to be the same to Char.

You don't know you need stuff till it's waved in front of your face, do you? We didn't buy anything, just looked. It kept Char happy, but I was pretty bored. Bored and dissatisfied, which is a bad combination, because yes, I'd like to have new tops, jeans, earrings, shoes, you name it, to glam up when I wanted, and not always look the same. Play at being Rosie Pickings, I suppose. But I can't, so I might as well forget it. No dosh, no threads!

On Tuesday lunchtime we had a cup of tea downtown in Freeman and Bennett's after Char had listened to me scraping a second place in the four-way fiddle class with my Beethoven 'Romance'. I hope you noticed the word 'scrape'. I thought I sounded awful, and was gobsmacked, not to say overjoyed, that I didn't come last. But the adjudicator (obviously deaf) said she thought my performance was 'really musical', and had 'moments of passion'. Or maybe I didn't hear her right. 'Moments of panic' might have been nearer the mark.

Over the Earl Grey, Char started to pump me about the meaning of (my!) life. I expect I was moaning about Ciarán and the dance school. Again.

'Why do you do it, then?' she asked, like I was a complete dumbo.

'Well, I like dancing... I like the feeling of being able to move,' I said.

'Yeah. But you can dance in clubs...' she replied.

'Can you?' I said, boggling a bit. I mean, let's get real here. Char's old for her year, 'cos she's fourteen already, and maybe if you were blind and it was a dark night, you could take her for sixteen at a pinch because of her size, but my birthday's not till February, and until I get some proper boobs and grow four inches, no doorman's going to let me into *The Blue Angel* or *The Bunker* or even the Year Eleven Ball! Anyway, not to ask.

'That kind of dancing's not the same,' I went.

'I don't get the difference,' she said. Which seemed so brainless to me, I didn't know where to begin.

'Well, for the first one you need technique and it's really hard. Can *you* do a *rond de jambe*? And the other – well, it's just a few steps and a bit of imagination. Isn't it?'

'But all the practice and stuff. Sounds to me like it's more trouble than it's worth...'

'It's great – when I've got the time. And if I didn't do it, I wouldn't ever get to perform. And if I didn't perform, I'd miss it badly. S'pose I'm a show-off. That's the honest truth!'

'So will there be more people watching your dance competitions than there were listening to the fiddle?'

The violin class had amassed an audience of two parents plus Char. Not even Everard had shown up, so Char had a point. What's with performing if no one's watching?

'Yeah,' I said doubtfully. 'Probably a few more...'

'Not exactly the wild applause of the adoring masses, then.'

'No.'

'Still don't get it! Is it, like, to please your mum?'

Back off, Char!

'No! She made me go when I was little, I suppose.'

'And what would she say if you told her you were giving up?'

Char had touched a raw nerve. I have to admit, I *have* thought about this.

'Yeah, she'd say she was disappointed, I guess...'

'Why?'

'Because she thinks it's good for me…'

'For deportment… for *poise*…' Char guffawed. 'That's what my mum used to say.'

I boggled again. Char *really* doesn't look like a dancer.

'You used to dance?' I tried not to sound surprised.

'Till I was eleven. Then I told my mum to stuff it. She just wanted to be able to brag to people about how her darling daughter did ballet, because she thought it sounded posh.' Char sounded very bitter. Just for a moment she had me pondering my mum and her motives.

Anyway, by all accounts, at that point rugby took over from ballet as far as Char was concerned.

On Tuesday evening, because Char says she never misses a home game, I was dragged along to Welford Road to watch the Leicester Tigers play Manchester's Sale Sharks. Her treat to me! Or some kind of revenge.

I don't understand the finer points of rugby, but it's not rocket science, is it? And I have to admit it was very exciting in a way I can't quite pin down. Char spent most of the evening screaming her head off, and eventually I joined in too, occasionally in the right places and for the right team. We'd persuaded Debs to take us, but she just buttoned up her fake fur and sat on her hands, restricting herself to comments about the desirability or otherwise of the players. The thing that fascinated me was their ears: twisted and swollen like modern sculptures.

'Imagine looking at *that* over the breakfast table every morning,' Debs murmured about one particularly fine example. Yup. I could see her point.

Where we were seated must have been right over the changing rooms, because every now and then the aroma of Deep Heat floated up from underneath, mingling with the smell from the hot dog stalls. Novel. And really not very nice.

Leicester won, which sent the crowd, including Char, into jumping-up-and-down ecstasy. I found myself comparing St Michael's Church to Welford Road's rugby ground. Maybe I could see now why St Michael's hadn't been all that strange to her. At both places Char was in the middle of crowds where she didn't know most people, at both there was raucous singing, and at both people were *worshipping* in different ways. The rugby was more exciting, but somehow seemed to me a bit pointless. Which, since Char had almost convinced me of the pointlessness of dancing too, and I was still cross I couldn't afford all those nice clothes I wanted, left me feeling rather empty as the week progressed.

I was still thinking about the rugby match on Thursday morning in the De Montfort Hall as we waited for the tap class to begin. At ten thirty in the morning the atmosphere was flat and lifeless. A handful of competitors' mums and siblings were scattered around the hall's large, lofty space, sprawling on the uncomfy chairs. Char was far away, deep down in a Californian ravine with the new Patricia Cornwell, digging up bodies. As we tappers were called to go back to the green room, there was an extra buzz while the hall began to fill up with six-year-old pixies and their entourages. The class immediately after us was the inter-school junior ballet ensemble, one of the big annual head-to-heads between Ciarán and Miss Bullen. There seemed to be an awful *lot* of pixies...

Whether I was just very chilled, or simply didn't care, I don't know, but I tapped amazingly well, though I say it myself. I simply blew them away. My music was 'All for the Best' from *Godspell*: great changes of tempo, and a really good wind-up to the end. I was so sensational, I won by miles.

'That was great,' said Char, abandoning California for a moment when I plonked myself on a chair beside her. 'You're *very* good, aren't you!'

'Thank you,' I said graciously.

'Fantastic, darling!' said Ciarán, passing by in a cloud of Chanel. A gaggle of pixies trailed behind her. Ciarán's hair was coloured poster-paint red and blue and piled up in a tower that added a foot to her height. 'That showed them!'

She meant 'that showed *her*!', i.e. Dora Bullen.

'Who is *she*?' said Char, in awed disgust at Ciarán. 'And where *does* she get her hair done?'

As Ciarán swept on towards the door leading backstage, Dora Bullen exited from the very same door and almost seized her by the throat. Bullen has a very deep, manly voice.

'I've been looking for you,' she growled menacingly. The hall went quiet as the two dinosaurs squared up. 'What do you mean by it?'

Ciarán looked blank. 'What?' she said, about as rudely as you can.

'This,' declared Bullen, like one of Char's detectives uncovering the carpet over a dead body. She flourished a large, dramatic hand at Ciarán's pixies, who cowered away. One started to cry quietly. 'Pixies!' she hissed. 'You stole our idea, Ciarán. I know you did. I can't believe even *you* would stoop so low...'

'Oh Dora, get a life!' said Ciarán, gathering the pixie band up and pushing them forward through the door. 'How many ideas are there in the world? Pixies one year, forest animals another. How long have you been doing this? Grow up!'

'I'm going to see the adjudicator,' Bullen hollered at Ciarán's back. 'You haven't heard the end of this!'

'You do that!' Ciarán snapped, and slammed the door behind her.

'Are they always like this?' Char asked, wide-eyed.

'Quite often,' I admitted.

The tap was the highlight of the week for me. I got a second in my jazz class, but didn't dance well. And I came nowhere in the ballet, which was a bit of a downer 'cos I thought that by my standards, I was smoking. Mum came down to watch.

'You looked really nice, dear,' she said consolingly.

At which Char glanced across at me, and made a kind of 'yuk' face. Or maybe it was a 'told-you-so' face. I'm not sure.

There was some more classic stuff from Ciarán and Dora during Friday. Ciarán was huffing and puffing that there'd been some heckling from the audience during my ballet class, though if anyone was having a go while I was dancing I didn't hear it, and nor did Mum. The music was playing way too loud.

'It's those two in the front row,' Ciarán said to me afterwards, pointing at a large woman in a shell suit and her daughter. 'I'll shut their gobs for them if they don't keep quiet.'

How nice!

Ciarán was confident of a first in the song and dance duet for the Harmon twins. She's confident about everything the Harmon twins do. In fact, she's confident they're going to be her first ex-pupils to make it to the West End and become international superstars. Well, OK, Stephen and Tricia are good for their age (11) but they're not that special – in my humble opinion.

Just after the ballet, while we were packing up to go home, and twenty minutes before the Harmons were supposed to strut their stuff, there was a kerfuffle. It was Ciarán marching down the hall to seize Dora Bullen by the short and curlies. In her wake followed Stephen and Tricia Harmon, looking dead embarrassed.

'Where are their costumes?' she went at Dora.

Dora Bullen ignored her, and went on yattering to her chums.

'Did you hear me? I said, where are their costumes? Or have you gone deaf?' Ciarán repeated.

Dora turned round and said as slowly and insultingly as she could, 'Ciarán dear, it's rude to shout. Now, what's your problem?'

'One of your little thieves has stolen these two's costumes. You've got five minutes to give them back or else...'

A low, barely audible rumble came from deep inside Dora Bullen, the first hint of a thunderstorm.

'I think you really should be careful before you use words like "steal" Ciaran. It's very offensive.'

'I don't care if it's offensive. Stealing's pretty offensive too. If they're not returned in the next five minutes, I'm going to dial 999!'

It was too good to miss. We sat back, even Mum, and watched as the two rivals went at each other hammer and tongs for a while before the festival organizer arrived and threatened them both with the red card. That shut them up. Eventually, it turned out someone's mum *had* walked off with the Harmons' costumes, because they were in an identical Top Shop bag to their own child's. Mystery solved.

'If I were you,' said Char afterwards, 'I would definitely look for some other outlet for my terpsichorean talent. It's a no-brainer. These people are a total waste of space, Abs. You know they are!'

That's all very well for Char to say, but the problem is, I still care what Ciarán thinks. And when she tells me as she did later that I '... did really well in the ballet... [*pause*]... for you, Abigail!', a part of me thinks she's a patronizing cow, but a part of me grows a bit. Which at five feet one is useful.

There was the strangest thing on the way home on Friday. As we were walking round to the multi-storey where Mum had left the car, a BMW mini whizzed round the Leicester one-way system, taking a corner on two wheels, and causing people crossing the road to jump for their lives. I caught only the most fleeting glimpse of the driver, whose head and shoulders were hunched over the steering wheel so that his greasy hair almost touched it, and it was on the tip of my tongue to say out loud, 'That's Eddie Finn!' But then I checked myself, because it was such a stupid thing to say, and it couldn't possibly have been.

But it really did look like Eddie!

Blog the Ninth
5 November

I've started scribbling these blogs before anyone else gets up on a Sunday morning. It saves people busting in, peering over my shoulder and asking nosey questions. Like, 'Who are *you* writing to? Got a boyfriend at last?' (Sneering, patronizing voice. Bog-breath over the shoulder. That'll be my brother then!)

No, Pete. Have you?

So here's me, the PC, a cup of Nescafé, and the dawn chorus.

Actually, even though the mornings are really dark now, I seem to be waking up earlier and earlier. So rather than just lying there worrying about the day ahead, I tend to get up and do stuff even when I've got school. I tried it before the poxy Year Eight exams last summer a couple of times, and it seemed to work for a while then. What with all the various after-school commitments, and getting something to eat, it's kind of hard to get homework done in the evening. And I've noticed my brain definitely works better after a sleep. Maybe that's why Dad naps so much. And I always thought it was laziness! Official! I'm becoming a morning person.

Originally the intention had been for Char to go back to Thornton Bramleigh on Saturday, but she threw me a bit by saying, 'Do you think I could stay till Sunday afternoon, Abs? Then I could come to church with you in the morning.'

I tried not to look disappointed. I know I should have been pleased she wanted to tag along, but the truth was I'd had enough of babysitting.

'Yeah. Yeah, sure! Erm… Char… The morning service won't be exactly like last Sunday evening…'

Which was an understatement. Sunday mornings at St Michael's are, like, vicars in funny clothes, choirboys, organs played moderately badly, people in suits and hats. You get the picture.

Church the way it is on the Christmas cards but without the holly, the mistletoe and the cosy glow. When I explained this, she said, 'That's cool!'

Oh, well! She couldn't say I hadn't warned her.

When I'm in church, I don't kneel down to pray. I don't quite know why. Maybe it's something to do with feeling uncomfortable and not being able to concentrate when my nose is bumping against the pew in front and my knees are sore. There's pride too. Why should God want me to grovel around on the floor? What does it do for him?

Anyway, the thing is, as soon as Matt the vicar was out of the traps with 'Let us pray', while I was sitting there trying to get a grip, Char had dropped straight down onto her kneeler, back ramrod straight, eyes closed, hands together in front of her lips. She looked beautiful actually. Peaceful. Even Char's friends would say that normally she's a bit of a lump, but just then she looked wonderfully graceful, like someone in a medieval painting. And she was working so hard at her praying, lips moving silently, crossing herself (where did *that* come from?), and concentrating fiercely in a very un-Char-like way.

I was so fascinated, wondering what was going on inside her head, that I forgot to pray myself. She must have felt me looking, and half turned towards me, smiling. I pretended I was being holy, meditating on the sculpture in the side aisle behind her.

Afterwards, as we were pushing past Matt and Adam at the door, she touched my arm and said quietly, 'Thank you. That was really lovely!'

'Who's that?' whispered Jana from somewhere behind me in the holy huddle on the church path, while Char was being chatted up by a churchwarden. I told her.

'Well done, you,' she said. Like it had been anything to do with me!

As soon as I walked through the school gates on Monday, there was Em. I'd called her at home twice during half-term to see if she wanted to come to the festival at the De Montfort with Char and me. The first time, I'd got her mum, and there'd been a stilted conversation finishing in the claim that Em 'wasn't available at the moment', while the background sound effects of running footsteps and suspicious rustling tended to suggest otherwise. The second time, we'd had a huffy exchange during which Em let me know she had much better (unspecified!) things to do than trail after me all half-term.

Now I did my bright and breezy, let's-forget-the-last-point-and-play-the-next thing.

'Hey, just look at you!'

Em was wearing a new puffa jacket so smart it was a security risk.

She sniffed but didn't actually reply, although as a concession she turned and walked half a pace behind me towards the lockers.

'Char gone home, then?' she said.

Here we go again, I thought.

'Yeah. Should think she's had enough of the Goodenoughs to last a lifetime,' I joked.

Em harrumphed.

'We could go skating on Wednesday... if you want,' I said tentatively. This was an olive branch so large it should've blocked the road. Em likes her skating a lot. Normally, I'd have to have my arm twisted off to get me anywhere near a rink. Recipe for broken bones and severed arteries, if you ask me.

'Don't mind,' she said airily, playing hard to get.

Oh, for heaven's sake! This really can't go on.

'I'll take that as a "yes" then, shall I?'

'If you like...'

I found Char at break and went straight to the point I should have tackled days – if not weeks – earlier.

'Char, I've *got* to tell Em about your situation at home. She's gone all mingy on me because she thinks I've dumped her for you.'

Char looked suitably horrified. 'That's awful,' she said. 'You two have been best mates for ever. Look, just forget about me. I can cope.'

'No you can't!' I said. 'It shouldn't have to be about choosing one person or the other. But it might help if you showed you trusted Em.'

'I do…' said Char, in a voice which made it clear she didn't.

'Well, think about it,' I said. 'It would help me big-time!'

So Char told Em the whole story that lunchtime, which was brave of her. The way Em was pumping me for extra gory details by phone later in the evening, I had the impression it really brightened up her day. Em does so like her goss. I hope getting Char to tell wasn't one big mistake! I was still worrying about Rosie Pickings.

Tuesday was the complete pits in oh so many ways.

There was me thinking I was the shoo-in to be Under 14 basketball captain. I promise you I've worked my little socks off this term. Despite everything else that's being going down, I've been a regular at Watkinson's practices, even when I was feeling grotty with the flu. I've worked on my skills. I've improved my speed. But hey, who gives one about any of that! Instead, Wazzo waltzes up to me at the end of practice and says, 'Well done, Abigail. Full marks for effort. You've really come on in the last few weeks!'

Like an idiot, there I was sitting on the metaphorical railway track, feeling so proud of myself, and thinking I was safe as houses. I never saw the train coming.

'Such a shame about your lack of inches…'

I was like, *What?*

'… But there it is. You're probably going to hate me for saying this, Abi – ' (*I do already, Miss Watkinson!*) ' – but basketball just isn't going to be your game, is it? And we've got such a strong squad this year. There'll be a lot of competition for places. So, Abi, I hope you won't find this disappointing…'

One of those moments when I'm not sure I'm hearing this…

'… but it's possible… may not get regular games next term… blah blah… got to expect… some of the other teams… very physical… blah blah… know you'll give Emily… full support…'

Emily? Emily Bradley? *That* Emily – the one who has difficulty catching a cold, let alone a basketball, and has all the speed and grace of a carthorse? And the leadership potential of same!

I didn't know what to say. So size *does* matter, then, despite what the magazines say. But isn't there a law against this sort of thing: race, gender, age, *height*? If there isn't, there should be.

And then, once we'd changed and were dragging our weary limbs homeward, the future prime minister and captain of the U14 pie-thrower team, The Right Honourable Dame Emily Bradley turns to me and says, 'Gonna have to pull out of skating tomorrow, Abs. Sorry!'

'Oh. Why?' I gave her the axe-murderer stare. I was still furious with Watkinson.

'Sally's invited me round to hers.'

'Sally Kennedy?'

'Yeah. Can't wait to see it. Sounds like it's a real deal rock palace.'

Sounded like a real deal pile of sour grapes and revenge to me. And this even *after* she knew the reason for me having Char to stay.

'Fine. Whatever. Another time.'

And I huffed off, with Em in my wake, 'cos even her dimwit brain had twigged I was really narked.

So much for loyalty. Before the start of this school year I couldn't have imagined *anything* ever coming between Em and me. But actually when it comes to the crunch, friendship is so fragile.

And *then*, hanging around outside the school gates were Tyler Dunn and some of his mates. Tyler's a Year Ten, and simply a horrible deviant. Loaded with pimples, pustules and testosterone, weighed down with a chip on his shoulder the size of the Empire State Building, you just know Tyler's got a great criminal future lined up.

He and his would-be gangsta sidekicks obviously had nothing better to do – no old ladies to rob, no walls to deface, no flies needing wings shredding – so they followed us down the street instead.

'Some of those posh kids who suck up to Dickson, innit?' I heard one of them say. Em and I tried not to quicken our step and give away the fact we were scared witless.

'Better watch out, ickle girls. That Dickson's a paedophile man.

They gonna put him away for that one day soon.'

Dirty laughs.

'Wanna come down the park? Get a better time wiv us than wiv Dickson, right?'

And so on and so on, with insulting references to our womanly shape, size, weight and so on. Or, in my case, lack of it.

After a hundred yards or so of wind-up, Em suddenly turned round, and faced them down. She was several inches taller than Tyler or his cronies. They stopped and leered up at her. But you could see they were surprised.

'Stop following us, OK? We've heard it all before, and it don't impress, right? So just push off and go bother someone else who cares more!'

And amazingly, after a few token insults to save face, they gave up with a final, 'See you some night soon, ladeez. You gonna miss us. You know you will!'

Maybe Wazzo's right. Maybe Em's the one with the leadership potential. I wouldn't have fronted up to Tyler the way she did. But for all that, we didn't part the best of friends.

And *then*, when I got in, Mum was in the foulest of moods. She looked grey, like she was going down with something, and obviously for some unspoken reason she'd had a lousy day too. She was at me as soon as I was through the door.

Didn't I know my room was like the council rubbish dump though less tidy would I vac through the whole house please *NOW* and no argument hadn't I noticed she was *INSANELY* busy too and had to cook dinner and couldn't do everything *WHERE WAS MY DAD* I looked a mess didn't I all my school clothes had stains or tears when was I going to do something about it I was the most scruffy of all her children even Pete which was absolutely saying something and didn't I understand how I was *LETTING THE FAMILY DOWN* wasn't it about time I faced up to my responsibilities I wasn't a little child any longer was I?

I did the vacuuming with a bad grace, bumping and grinding

round the furniture, so she'd know I'd got the hump. There was a nasty, irritated vibe all evening. Then, after supper, I stomped upstairs and had a wail into my pillow because nothing in the world was fair and no one was listening to ME! I junked homework for the night, went to bed early, couldn't sleep and got up at 5.30 the next morning to do what had to be done, resentful and feeling like death.

If I'm honest, Mum's been a pain all week. Not just with me either, so I'll try not to take it personally. Everyone's copped it at some point, Dad included. Maybe it's the menopause. More likely it's the parish office. Matt the vicar doesn't seem to treat her with respect, dropping piles of work on her without warning. Perhaps it's time to give up. Or do we need the dosh? I don't know. I can't ask.

Saturday was the big A Club outing of the term, to the Tate Modern art gallery in London. It was also Guy Fawkes Night, but since we don't do that at the Goodenoughs, I was happy with the thought I could watch everyone else's through the windows of the minibus on the way home up the M1.

There were a dozen kids in total (the seven regular A Clubbers plus four or five art boffs), AD and Zoe Hughes, who got to do the driving, which surprised me. I'd have thought AD's ego would never cope with that. Obviously he's more liberated than I thought.

Em sat next to Sally, still thick as thieves after an evening in Sally's whizzy world. I sat with Char on one side and Syl on the other. I happened to mention to Char about how scratchy Mum had been with everyone during the week.

'I'm not the person to talk to about parents, am I?' she said.

'No,' I answered, suddenly feeling bad because my problem was so obviously minuscule compared with hers.

'I mean, once it wouldn't have crossed my mind, but now I think how *can* people stay together for ever?' she said, like this was a complete bald statement of fact.

And so I had an 'Oh my God' moment, which practically lifted me off the bus-seat. Because it had never occurred to me that the problem might be something between Mum and Dad. Then, like you do, thinking back over little things of the past few weeks, bits of niggle, odd comments, in five minutes I'd convinced myself that there couldn't be any other reason for Mum's moods. Mum and Dad must be splitting up.

Fortunately, we were just arriving in the outskirts of London, and the fact we were just getting lost because of AD's incompetent navigating took my mind off the Goodenoughs for the moment. Well, that and Eddie Finn's inane chat-up lines from the seat behind us, which gave Char a gut-busting attack of the giggles.

'He *fancies* you?' she whispered incredulously.

'I know,' I whispered back, as she collapsed into mirth again. *Very* funny. Not.

We ate our sandwiches by the River Thames near Waterloo, watching the boats go by. They were mostly tourist jobs with glass roofs, though there were a couple of strings of sad, empty barges, and a small black motorboat marked, 'Police', which must have had a learner driver on board from the way it was karooming about on the water.

The sun was warm on our faces and the sky was a cloudless, but slightly smoky, blue.

AD took us up on to Waterloo Bridge.

'I don't care what anyone says,' he shouted over the traffic noise. 'This is one of the best views in the world.'

The Goodenoughs don't come to London very much: maybe only once or twice a year, but I believe him. The way the river sweeps round just there, and you can see the famous Houses of Parliament with Big Ben (the real one, not the Leicester version!) in one direction, and St Paul's surrounded by modern city buildings like the Gherkin in the other, is so brilliant. It makes me feel amazed to think that of all the places I could have been born in the world, African townships, South American jungles, Russian steppes, I got delivered to Britain. Wow! I felt better just standing there.

It didn't impress some of the others though.

'Think of all the terrorists,' said Drew.

'Don't like big cities,' said Em. 'Look at the pollution!'

Well, there were some unmentionable things floating around in the water, as Eddie had been quick to point out during lunch. Some connections I do not want to make!

'My feet hurt,' said Sally. Daft girl. We'd only walked two hundred yards. Of course her feet hurt, on account of the stupid pointy shoes she'd stuck on them!

'No soul, some people,' hollered AD above the traffic.

Talking of buildings, the Tate Modern is pretty spectacular too. You'd think an old power station would be the last place you'd plonk an art gallery, but it's a stroke of genius. When we walked into the Turbine Hall near the entrance, it was Drew's turn to go 'Wow'.

The roof stretches far above you, higher than a cathedral, and there was an art installation filling it which reminded me a cross between penny-farthing bicycles and a space station, huge metal wheels turning and falling above our heads, while a soundtrack like electronic seagulls ebbed and flowed around us. Eddie seemed especially fascinated, standing there on one leg, head on one side, eyes following the track of the spinning metal.

After that, I thought what was actually hanging in the galleries was an anticlimax. It was a good thing I had Char with me to tell me what I was looking at. She seems to know everything there is to know about art.

AD said there was no point in all sticking together, that you couldn't get anything from a place like this as a group and he was sure he could trust us, but Going Outside was strictly forbidden. I think he just wanted an hour or so with Hughesey. He probably knew a bar where they could cuddle up over a Malibu.

So we buzzed around the various rooms for a while, looking at things that were recognizable as pictures, and other things that looked like piles of rubbish, and even on one or two occasions things resembling the stuff Eddie had noticed floating in the Thames.

Eddie had tagged along with Char and me, and that was OK, since he was mostly no trouble, apart from the occasional, inane remark. Then suddenly, he wasn't there.

'Where's Eddie gone?' I asked.

'*I* dunno,' said Char, 'He's your boyfriend, not mine.'

'Oh, shut up, Char,' I said. I immediately had this sixth sense that something wasn't right, like a tingling in the ears.

'I think we ought to look for him.' I knew it was a daft thing to say.

'Oh, leave it out, Abs,' went Char, who was well into the art, and didn't want her fun disturbed by the idiot Eddie. 'He's probably just gone to the bog or something. And before you suggest it, I'm not chasing into the gents to see if he's all right.'

'I'm going to check in the Turbine Hall. Eddie seemed very keen on all that,' I said.

'OK, well, I'm not going anywhere. You can find me here,' Char called after my back as I made for the escalators.

Eddie wasn't in the Turbine Hall, but Drew and Em were, squatting on the floor. They'd had all the art they could take for one day.

'Seen Eddie?' I panted.

'Yeah, a few moments ago. He went that way, I think...' Drew seemed not to understand my anxiety, while at the same time he was waving his arm towards the gallery front doors. Illogical!

'Eddie really fancies you, doesn't he?' went Em.

'Don't start that!' I said sharply. 'Look, don't ask me why, 'cos I really shouldn't care, but I'm worried about him. Drew, you don't think he was planning to go outside, despite what AD said?'

'The bookshop?' said Drew. The bookshop was by the entrance.

'Eddie? In a bookshop? Nah!' drawled Em.

'Well, stop gabbing, and let's go look!' I more or less heaved the two of them to a standing position.

No Eddie. Not in the bookshop.

'I want to check by the river,' I said.

'AD'll kill you!' Em looked genuinely shocked. I'm normally the goody-two-shoes law-abiding one. 'And anyway, what harm do you think Eddie can possibly come to?'

'Got a bad feeling. Can't explain it.'

'OK,' sighed Drew. 'One out, all out! Eddie's a good cause. If Abs goes on her own, all the doodah hits her fan. If the three of us go, it spreads the load.' What a way with words.

Em looked doubtful, but tagged along, alternately dawdling and trotting, throwing nervous glances over her shoulder in case we were spotted by AD or Hughesey.

There was a swarm of Japanese tourists on the walkway beside the river, and a steady procession of joggers. No Eddie.

'Round the back,' I shouted, and headed out into London at a slow jog myself, not giving the other two time to argue. There were small streets with cars on either side in the parking bays. We went one block downriver. Still no Eddie. I turned to the south.

'Hey, slow down, Abs. Where are you going?' came a distant chorus of two from behind me around the corner.

And then, bullseye! As if we'd been supernaturally drawn to him, *there* was Eddie, a hundred metres away up the street. He was walking close to the cars, so near that his hand trailed along their paintwork on his left-hand side. Suddenly, even as I watched, he stopped and felt the handle of one of them, testing it to see if it would open. It did, and in a flash Eddie had disappeared inside.

I sprinted up the street, till I was parallel with him. He was crouched down inside a BMW similar to the one I'd seen being driven in Leicester. So that must have been Eddie too! His head was down under the steering wheel as he fiddled with wires, and he didn't see me until I knocked on the car window. He nearly went straight through the the BMW's multicoloured roof in shock. When he'd landed again, and registered it was only me, he went rigid for a second, skin ghostly white, eyes staring. And then, after a suspended few seconds in which I was sure a posse of coppers would nee-naw their way up the street and cart us off to the local nick, Eddie accepted he was rumbled, and started to exit the BMW. I half pulled him out, pushing the car door shut with my bum. No fingerprints. Eddie already had me thinking like a crim.

By now, the other two had caught up with us.

'Don't ask,' I said. 'Let's just get him out of here.'

We were just in time. As we sprinted back towards the river which, thinking about it now, wasn't the cleverest thing to do (walking would have been a lot wiser!), a posh-looking young couple holding each other and matching golf umbrellas in their hands turned into the street. You just knew they were the BMW's owners. They glanced curiously at us as we dashed past.

'Did you leave your brain in Leicester?' I gasped, hyperventilating as we reached the plaza by the Tate. 'What on earth d'you think you're doing, Eddie?'

'You gonna shop me, then?' His eyes were sullen, his voice small and anxious.

'What do you think?' I replied. Then, sounding like my mum, 'Not that you don't deserve it!'

Eddie shrugged his shoulders. 'Up to you, innit!' he muttered glumly.

'No, of course we won't shop you,' I said, wondering whether I really meant it, and what the prison sentence was for aiding and abetting a car thief.

We walked into the Tate, and ran slap bang into AD and Hughesey.

'Where have you been?' AD said sternly.

'We... We just went out to get some air,' Drew stuttered. 'Em felt faint... didn't you, Em?'

'Uh... yeah, yeah, that's right,' she went, slightly slow to cotton on, which was actually quite a helpful effect. 'Really bad. The room was like, spinning, up there.'

Em's lie was reasonably convincing, but we *all* looked hot and dishevelled. I shouldn't think AD bought it for one moment.

'Hmm. Didn't I expressly tell you not to go outside? I thought you were all mature enough to be trusted, and I'm very disappointed,' he chuntered crossly. 'And why did it take all four of you to go? I'd have expected better. Have you any idea what they'd do to Miss Hughes and me if anything were to happen to you?' And he singled me out for the big stare, like it was obviously all my fault. Thank you *so* much! Why me?

AD knew he'd had the wool pulled over his eyes about something, but he didn't know what, so the atmosphere between him and us in

116

the minibus back to Leicester stayed tense. This time AD drove, concentrating fiercely through the evening traffic. From where I sat, I could see Hughesey's hand resting softly on his knee. As we waited for a traffic jam to clear, she smoothed his hunched shoulders, trying to persuade him to relax. He turned and smiled at her, a nice, open, un-AD-like smile. They seemed very much a couple.

As we hurtled up the motorway, there was plenty of time to watch the fireworks outside, and think. About Mum and Dad. About the A Club. Maybe AD was regretting the whole idea. We weren't much of a success for him so far, were we? More likely to get him sacked than make his fortune!

Foul week. Horrible week. Worst-ever week. In fact, a week so bad, I don't want to talk about it, full stop.

But I'd better write *something*, so try this for size. In History this week we were discussing the way people's minds change after a war. They get sick of killing each other, and having ration books, so they chuck out the old government, and decide to do things differently. Well, apparently that's what happened in 1945 after World War II. And since I feel like I've been in a war zone all week, here's my revolution. This is the way the world should be:

Abi's manifesto

1) People should *always* be honest with each other. I can't stand it when people say one thing to your face, when you know they're saying something else behind your back. What's the point? The truth always comes out eventually.

2) Fighting's a waste of time. It *never* improves things. So don't do it. That means kids and adults too.

3) Listen up, parents! *You* hold all the cards. *You're* the ones with the money. *You're* the ones who can do what they like. *You're* the ones who are supposed to take care of *us*. Not the other way round.

4) Listen up, teachers! You're taking money for teaching, aren't you? OK, I know you have stuff to put up with, and I definitely wouldn't want to teach Tyler Dunn and his crew. But if you're teaching me, well, I'm just a girl whose intentions are good, so put the power

trips and the aggro in the cupboard and leave them there. Pupils have feelings too.

5) For all adults everywhere. Stop dodging questions! It's no good telling people all their problems will go away if they become good little Christians. I want to believe in God, and most days I do. But I still don't see why God couldn't have made a world where there wasn't unhappiness and suffering. Babies don't have to die of starvation. People don't have to drown in floods. Not if there's a God who can do anything.

6) As far as prime ministers and presidents and those sorts of people go, just sort it out, guys! There's enough food in the world for everybody. So make sure it gets to the people who need it. Then there wouldn't be any war. Simple. If I can work it out, why can't you?

OK, maybe I do want to talk about this week.

I'm gobsmacked at the way Em's behaved, I really am. I feel let down. But the thing is, *how* did Em mean what she said? And should I trust Sally anyway?

Explain, Abi!

I haven't worked Sally Kennedy out. She always comes on very friendly and open, but there's more to it than that. Sometimes it's like she's desperate to be everyone's friend.

There I was, trying to get a few minutes to myself in the library at Willowmede on Tuesday morning, revising for a Physics test, when Sally sidled up to me, ignoring the fact I was obviously trying to work.

'How's Char?' she said for starters.

Straight away, warning bells rang.

'What do you mean?' I asked suspiciously.

'You know… All the stuff at home…'

Sally wasn't supposed to know. *How* did she know?

'OK,' I said guardedly. 'At least, I think so.'

'I thought you'd be up to date. Being so close and that.'

I was a bit sharp. 'It's not any of our business, is it?'

Sally shrugged. 'I've been there, that's all,' she said. 'Parents splitting. That kind of stuff. I know what it's like. Anyway, it's good Char's got you...'

'Excuse me,' I interrupted, 'But how do you know about this? Did Em tell you?'

'Yeah,' said Sally casually, like this was any other goss.

'Well, she shouldn't have done.'

Sally looked put out. 'Well, I'm sorry!' she pouted. 'Only taking an interest, wasn't I? Just because you two have got a thing going...'

'I beg your pardon. Which two? What sort of *thing*?'

'You and Char. Well, that's what Em said.'

'What *exactly* did Em say?'

By now, Sally could see I was riled, and she tried to back off. Too late.

'Come on Sally, I want to know. Tell me. What did Em say?'

'Well, I didn't believe her, of course... not like that...'

'Yeah?'

'OK. Look, Em said Char had a crush on you. Like a sort of lesbo thing?'

I was so angry, I was speechless.

I've avoided Em all week, so she'll know there's something up. Come to think of it, she's avoided me too, which has got to be down to guilt. How could she say that, even as a joke?

The thing with Sally and Em. It's a pinprick. I know that. It pales into insignificance beside Mum and Dad.

I'm trying to be as rational as I can, to imagine I'm a detective assembling the evidence, to keep my feelings out of it. But in the end, my rational, calm, detective conclusion is that Char must be right. It's obvious Mum and Dad have got issues, big ones. But when is 'big' big enough to destroy a marriage?

It's not like there've been massive rows and smashed crockery.

But two or three nights, I've lain in bed straining my ears till the small hours of the morning, while Mum and Dad have talked and talked. Not sweet, soft voices, but urgent, anxious ones, never loud enough for me to hear what's actually been said, but quite loud enough to know that these are two very unhappy, disagreeing people.

I can't tell you what it does to me inside. It ties knots in my stomach. It makes the blood pump and throb round my head. It makes me bury my head in the duvet one moment so I can't hear, and then the next moment creep out of bed to open the bedroom door a crack so I can hear better.

In the morning, Mum invariably comes to breakfast looking awful, grey and worn out. Her hair's straggly and she's barely making an effort to look presentable when she drags herself off to the parish office or the prison. Dad makes a show of being anxious about her, but she's always pushing him away. The rest of the time he's on another planet, so vague you can't get any sense out of him at all. And both of them have been pretty nasty to me and Pete. At least they agree on that.

I can't believe how quickly things have changed. There wasn't a hint of this a month ago. Is one of them having an affair? And if so, how? When? Who with? Mum and Matt the vicar? Or Adam?

I can't bear it. We're going to end up in the papers, just like the Ellisons.

What with no sleep during the first half of each night eavesdropping on M & D, and the alarm drilling a hole in my head at five every morning so I can summon up the energy for some homework, I've been knackered when I've got to school, which, quite apart from the Em factor, hasn't been a bunch of fun.

To avoid Em, I walked home with Drew on Wednesday, while he droned on about how he was training himself to improve his memory. I wasn't listening really, still thinking about Em and what a pig she'd been.

'So say I've got to remember all the cars on that garage forecourt...' he was going, pointing at a collection of clapped-out old bangers on the other side of the road.

'You sound like Eddie Finn,' I muttered, brain on autopilot. 'Why would you want to do that?'

He ignored me.

'… So what I do is, I think of each one with a sort of number on its roof, like they have on a golf course… you know, for each hole… or maybe a die… like for snakes and ladders?… though perhaps not with dots on… 'cos that would be confusing… perhaps more like the route number on a bus…'

As Drew's monologue meandered pointlessly on, Tyler Dunn and two of his fat sidekicks emerged from an alley up ahead. They saw us, checked, and leant against the wall, leering, waiting for us to draw level with them.

'… Anyway, I consciously visualize each car in turn, and then if I want to remember the whole garage, all I have to do…'

'Just shut up a moment Drew,' I hissed. 'Look, it's Tyler Dunn.'

'So? Am I boring you?'

'He's probably going to give us grief…'

'Why?'

'Why does the sun shine, Drew? I don't know. It's just what Tyler does, isn't it?'

We were still twenty yards away when Tyler started.

'Dickson's ickle girlfriend,' he called.

'She's two-timing 'im, man, innit?' answered fat boy one.

'Watch out, little girl, we're gonna tell. Put you in big trouble,' fat boy two chirruped.

'Blown out for lickle ginger nuts. Don't think Dickson'll dig that…'

I pulled my bag off the shoulder nearest to them and the wall, gripping it tightly. The Tyler posse moved out to block the path.

'What you goin' to pay so we don't grass you up?'

It was a stand-off. As Drew and I moved this way and that to go through or round them, so they sidestepped and stood in our way. The street was empty of people. Each of Tyler's crew was much bigger than Drew and me put together.

'Don't be stupid,' I said feebly. 'Let us through.'

'If you didn't been eatin' curry or nuffin', a kiss would do...' smirked Tyler. 'Then, when you paid, you can go...'

'... But you gotta kiss all three of us,' cackled FB1.

'Better put some gum in yo' mouth, man. Yo' breath smells evil!' went FB2 to his mate.

'Put a brick in it,' said Drew, suddenly roused to action, 'I s'pose you think it's smart, picking on someone half your size.'

For the record, Drew is three inches taller than me. And he's three inches shorter and several hundred pounds lighter than Tyler. I never exaggerate.

'Leave it, Drew,' I muttered. 'It won't help.' Drew's parents had probably fed him stuff about standing up to bullies, like parents generally do when they haven't been to school for thirty years.

But Drew took a step forward, and made as if to move FB1 aside with his arm to create a gap for us to go through. FB1 took the arm, spinning Drew round and forcing it up Drew's back. He twisted the wrist until Drew gave a yelp of real pain.

'Yo' stupid or what?' said the thug.

FB2 casually kicked Drew's legs away from under him just as FB1 let go. As Drew went down an arm flailed out and struck FB2 a glancing blow on the chin, more by accident then design. FB1 swore and caught Drew, who was on his way down to the pavement, with a punch to the nose. Drew's face was already leaking blood as he hit the floor. With perfect timing, Tyler captured the moment for posterity on his mobile phone's camera.

In the distance, I saw a burly-looking middle-aged man turning the corner. Tyler caught sight of him too, snapped the mobile shut, and whistled his cronies away. But before they retreated up the alley to find whichever stones they'd crawled out from under, FB2 took Drew's rucksack and hurled it over the high red brick wall beside us.

'I'll shop you. I will!' I shouted, mad with frustration, just not caring any more.

'You do, and we'll find you,' FB2 grated. 'And *then* you'll be sorry.'

The burly bloke walked on past, giving us a dirty look as he went, like it was our fault Drew had got beaten up. He didn't say a dicky bird, even though he must have been able to see Drew was hurt. Still, maybe he saved us from worse. Drew eventually hobbled home, school sweatshirt grubby, shirt and trousers torn. But first we had to endure the hassle of finding the house behind the wall, and asking permission to retrieve the rucksack, which had come open in the course of its aerial journey, scattering papers and pens (how many does a boy need?) over half of Leicestershire.

'Can you remember everything that was in the bag?' I said, still shaking slightly from the shock.

'Ha ha!' Drew winced, clutching a bloodied handkerchief to his nose. 'So you were listening, then! And no, every pen doesn't have its own sodding number!'

The next morning I started a really painful period, so bad I thought at first I wouldn't make it into Willowmede. Cue Mum, looking like Mrs Death herself, minus hood and sickle, with her happy thought for the day. 'Might as well just used to it. You're stuck with it till you're fifty, give or take. And when it stops happening, you'll know you're old. Or on the other hand...'

And she suddenly stopped midstream, like the thought I might ever get pregnant (and therefore she might be a grandma!) was just too much to take.

So, doped up on painkillers (which I hate taking unless I have to) and, panicking I'd run slap bang into Tyler, I trailed into school.

Drew's nose looked bigger than it usually did. The left cheek beside it was bruised, and a scab of dried blood was obvious under one nostril. At least he had the consolation of being able to say when questioned, 'Oh... a bit of a run-in with Tyler...' in a nonch kind of way. Whereas I just felt bad that if he hadn't walked home with me, it wouldn't have happened. Em was all over him, needless to say. Char too. And neither of them seemed interested *I'd* been there at all.

At lunchtime, AD came and found me moping over a radiator.

'Can you spare me a minute or two, please, Abigail?' he said. *Ouch*, I thought. *Full name. Must be bad news. What have I done now?*

Depending on the clothes he's wearing, AD seems to morph from one personality to another, like a shape-shifter in Star Trek. Today I was in conference with Mr Efficiency because he was in the grey chalk-striped power suit. On Monday I might have been swapping jokes with Mr Entertainer – bright red designer jacket. Tuesday I could have been down and rapping with Mr Cool – leather jacket and turtleneck. That's *his* idea of cool, not mine, you understand!

'Come in... You can leave the door open...' he said when we'd climbed the stairs to AD's cubbyhole office. Ridiculous, but I suppose we can't be shut in there alone without a chaperone.

I looked at him nervously, expecting recriminations after the Eddie thing at the Tate.

'Abi, you remember the community project I talked about at the beginning of term?'

I remembered the thumbs-down reaction it got from the A Clubbers and just knew I wasn't going to like what was coming next. My stomach and head were competing to see which could be the most painful, with alternate aches and throbs.

'I have a friend who works with special needs kids,' AD said. 'Do you know what I mean, Abi?'

I said I did.

'Actually, she co-ordinates work by teachers all over the county. In a way she's trying to do for kids with mental and physical disabilities what I'm doing for you. Because, in a way, the A Clubbers are special needs kids too. Understand?'

Fair comment. We're all pretty special, I'd say!

'So I've booked the school theatre for the Saturday after term ends. What I want you to do – *us* to do – is put on a Christmas concert for about a hundred and fifty children and their parents, plus the general public. I thought any money we raise could go to help send British athletes to the next Paralympics. What do you think?'

The cheek of the bloke. I mean, what about consultation, participation and all the other -ations? You don't just waltz in and tell a bunch of people to do something like this, without asking them if they're up for it. Or had I made a mistake and the army had taken over Willowmede in an overnight coup?

How do you tell a teacher his idea stinks?

'There's not much time, is there, sir?' I was trying the tactful approach.

'Oh come on, Abi, this is the end of term we're talking about. Weeks away!'

'Just over five weeks away actually, sir. Starting now to sort out the publicity, and organize the front of house? I was just thinking of Dame Jessica's lecture...'

'Well, that was a learning experience for all of us. I'm sure you'll be much better prepared this time.'

I liked the 'you'll' bit. Maybe I was going gaga with the pain, but I thought what happened was that *we* tried to rescue him from *his* rubbish preparation.

'And who's going to perform in the concert, sir?'

'I thought that would be safe in your hands, Abi.'

'Like what exactly, sir?' It was hard not to sound rude.

'Well there's... and then there's... well... you're the expert, Abi... with all your dancing and singing. I'd have thought it'd be easy for you to knock something up...'

Knock something up... **Knock something up?** The man clearly hadn't a clue.

My stomach was aching, my legs were aching, and my head was just about splitting apart. It was as if all the rubbish from other people's lives was being pressed down on my brain. They were cramming more into this dustbin than would go. Teachers, parents, friends; all competing to see how much of their unwanted stuff they could unload onto me, shouting, *Just do this Abs... What I need is... How do you?... Why can't you?...'*

I let them all scream for a while. And then, from somewhere deep inside me, I summoned up the energy to yell *'Shut up'*. But not out loud. AD didn't hear a thing.

'I can't take it on, sir,' I said, and at this point I was very calm, very logical. 'I simply haven't got the time. If I do anything else, my regular schoolwork just won't get done.'

There was an ominous silence. Mr Efficiency was absorbing this inconvenient information.

'I'm very disappointed, Abigail,' he intoned sonorously, before gradually working up a head of steam. 'I really am. You see, I don't think you understand. We – teachers, I mean – are very happy to give up our time – go the extra mile – for students like yourself. We want to see you do well. We want you to have the opportunities you might not otherwise access. That's why we spend our weekends taking you to galleries, running events, planning ways to stretch your minds. And sometimes it seems as if we get no thanks for it. Students choose only to do what they want. They play for themselves, not the team. We turn a blind eye when they make mistakes – do I need to mention last Saturday? – but they don't respond in kind. I mean, maybe we should have told your parents about the blatant disobedience. Maybe we should have said "never again". But did we? No! We forgot it, and moved on. And this is the thanks we get. I think it's about time you accepted a bit of responsibility, Abi. Because, you know, this is what adult life is going to be like. It's difficult. It's hard work. It's sleepless nights and early mornings. You've just got to shape up and cope. Really you have.'

I knew my eyes had been filling up with tears during this tirade. Now I struggled to hold them back, determined not to give AD the satisfaction. What sanctimonious, unfair, unsympathetic rubbish! There was even a hint of blackmail. In the end, what was the difference between him and Tyler? Both of them were bullies, and both of them would do everything they could to get what they wanted.

'I'm sorry, sir,' I said, standing up. 'I think it's *you* who doesn't understand. You don't know the first thing about me and my life. Or the other A Clubbers. You don't know how hard we work. You don't know the pressures we're under. You just see the bit between nine and four.'

'Oh, I think I do,' AD said, with a smug, knowing smile. 'You forget I was a school student too, not so long ago…'

'Well, maybe things have changed since then. I was up at five this morning to do my homework. And this weekend I'll probably have only a few hours off to please myself – ' (bit of an exaggeration, but hey, I was steaming) ' – but don't worry. We'll make your show happen. Leave it with us. Since you've promised the kids. Don't give it another thought.'

And I walked out. And then burst into tears. I hate it when I see kids dissing parents or teachers for no reason. But surely, if a grown-up's completely out of order, we shouldn't just have to stand there and take it? Is that fair?

I wagged afternoon school. OK, I didn't just walk out without telling anyone. What I actually did was to go and find Zoe Hughes and tell her I was having a real bad time of the month, and I couldn't say anything to Dr Dickson because I was too embarrassed. That way I thought I could get some space, and she'd probably tell him and then he'd feel guilty as hell for upsetting me.

Hughesey looked concerned, like she mostly does. Concerned, pale and gentle. I could talk to Zoe Hughes. She should be year head, not AD. I can't understand what she sees in him. 'Yeah,' she said, looking me carefully up and down. 'Yeah, Abi, that's fine. Parents at home?'

I nodded.

'Take care, then!'

But I didn't go home. I went and sat by the canal in the freezing cold, and thought about throwing myself in and ending it all. Seriously! At one point I stood on the wooden edge, balancing on my toes, imagining what it would be like to fall forward and just let go. And then, behind me, I heard a curious voice saying softly, 'Abi?'

It was Jana.

Blog the Eleventh
20 November

There's something very mysterious about Jana. Not to look at. She's a small, rather ordinary woman, with straight, dark, pageboy hair. About 35? Usually no make-up. Always wears very quiet clothes. Black. Brown. Blue jeans and a crisp white shirt if she's feeling jazzy. Never draws attention to herself. Doesn't have a bloke, that I've ever seen. Lives alone in a house that's spotlessly clean, with everything stripped to the bone. No ornaments, no luxuries. Enough furniture, enough food. Enough, but never more than enough. Horribly organized. And when she wants to be, which is, like, usually, Jana's incredibly still and calm. The effect when she's in company, the way she is sometimes with Tomorrow's People, can be to make *us* as focused and chilled as she is. It's the power of silence. I'm not saying she's not fun, because she definitely can be, but what I've described to you is Jana's default.

It seemed like a kind of magic when she turned up on the canal towpath. I mean, what were the chances of it happening, that she and I should both zero in on the same bench one particular freezing Friday afternoon at two fifteen? Especially since I wasn't meant to be there and should have been at home in bed, at least, as far as Zoe Hughes knew.

Jana spoke my name and there she was, as if she'd simply materialized out of thin air. A guardian angel!

But all the guardian angel said, (instead of 'Lo, I bring you tidings from Almighty God' or something) was, 'Hey Abs!', like this was perfectly normal, me balancing on the edge of the water, thinking about ending it all. I wobbled, and she giggled, 'Don't fall in, then!'

I didn't see the joke. I guess I was feeling too crumpled and sorry for myself.

129

'Coffee?' she asked, and because St Michael's was on the way home and the church's old-ladies-with-hats serve tea and cake every afternoon to anyone who'll risk going in, we went and sat at one of the tables in the church hall. It was sweltering in there; about fifty degrees hotter than it had been by the canal.

I know the way it can be with Jana. She earns her money from being a counsellor. That means people pay to talk to her (nice job!), and she helps them sort themselves out by making space for them to say what's on their mind. If you're not careful, you can easily find yourself gabbing to Jana the kind of stuff you'd rather keep quiet.

While we recovered from frostbite by warming our hands on the church's coffee mugs, she asked casually, 'How *are* things, then?'

But I was wary, my body still ached, and I wasn't ready to give her the skinny yet. Mum and Dad, Em, Char, Rosie Pickings, AD and the A Club stuff, even Drew and Eddie and Ciarán - everything was jumbled in my head, every set of problems tumbling over the next like clothes in a washing machine. I wouldn't have known where to start. So we swapped inane drivel for a while, though I was so zomboid, she must have guessed I was under some kind of mega-stress. Plus, why wasn't I in school? But tactfully she didn't go there.

'How's your friend, Char?' she asked at one point.

'OK... 'Ish!'

'Bringing her on Sunday evening?'

I suppose it had sort of crossed my mind. Every year, Tomorrow's People have a 'Fireworks and Prayer' party, and this Sunday was it. Should have been the previous week of course, but there'd been some mess-up with the church diary. A visiting bishop, I think.

The idea's quite groovy, in a religious sort of way. Jana buys one nice showy firework for each person. Then in turn we each have a chance to say what we'd like the group to pray for, and while our firework whizzes and fizzes and shoots coloured stuff around the sky, we all pray as hard as we can for that person's thing. Jana's brilliant at creating little ceremonies, and as ceremonies go, this one's pretty smart.

'Might be too late to ask...' I said defensively.

'Pity!' said Jana, which sharpened up a pang of guilt, like I needed some more of *that* just then.

'Might be a bit much for her?' I tried. 'A bit... holy... you know?'

Jana pulled a face as if to say, *'Maybe. Maybe not...'*

The truth was, I wanted the time for me and my thoughts. I'd had it up to *there* with other people's problems.

Perhaps it was the coffee, or the church hall heat, or maybe it was a sympathetic listening ear, but an hour with Jana and my period pain began to subside. A small miracle, Jana would have said, if I'd let on.

However, after the whole of the following weekend doing nothing much more than *thinking* (i.e. worrying!), I was well wired by the time Fireworks and Prayer came round. Yeah, all right, I'll admit it, I'd been a complete pain in the bum, moping round the house and not settling to anything. The general Goodenough vibe didn't help. Pete was out at footie most of both days, playing or watching, and since neither Debs nor Hannah put in an appearance, it was mostly me, Mum and Dad, all trying to avoid each other. When the point of 'do I stay or do I go?' came, Mum had to nag me into putting in an appearance.

'Oh, for heaven's sake,' she said. 'Make up your mind, and go. I don't know what's the matter with you these days, Abi!'

I almost told her exactly what the matter was, but somehow at the last moment my tongue became glued to my mouth and wouldn't come unstuck.

As I walked down to Jana's house, I replayed Friday afternoon and already felt stupid and ashamed. Had I really meant to throw myself into the sludgy green canal? Of course I hadn't. If by any chance I *had* accidentally toppled in, I'd have instantly been treading water like crazy to avoid the slightest drop of grade A toxic canal waste passing my lips. I'd been a right little drama queen and I knew it.

Jana left my firework till last. They always have one, but *only* one rocket. Apparently, this year the rocket had my name on it.

'What's on *your* mind, Abi?' said Jana finally, which is her formula for asking what you want to pray for. Most people, bother them, had been amazingly, horribly worthy. There'd been prayers for peace in the world, and freedom from hunger. There'd been yucky stories about aunties with multiple sclerosis, and brothers abroad with the army. And when we weren't worthy we were trivial. We'd even asked God for the safe return of wet Kayleigh's lost cat, Ferdinand, while a Roman candle went berserk over the neighbours' gardens, which struck me as amusing. Exactly the kind of thing to make the average cat run away and hide, I'd have thought. And all the while, waiting my turn, I was going quietly mental, my fuse burning down with every resentful second, 'cos *I* didn't have anything the least worthy to hit God with.

So, when it came to my big moment, I was tongue-glued again. My brain completely shut down. I shook my head violently, swallowed, sighed, and then eventually blurted out, like a moron with an attitude problem, 'All right, then. Me. If you insist. Me! If you want to pray for something, pray for me! OK?'

Jana's dead cool. She didn't blink. Despite the fact I'd pretty well screamed the last 'OK', she just said quietly, as if this was perfectly normal, 'That's fine. All right everyone, here we go. A prayer for Abi. Let's pray for peace for Abi…'

She and Dave, one of the Tomorrow's People parents, had lit everyone else's fireworks, but as a privilege for the oldest, Jana gave me a taper to launch the rocket myself.

I checked with her to make sure I hadn't misunderstood this breach of health and safety.

'It's OK. Go ahead,' she said encouragingly, and I scuttled forward to the ramp Dave had constructed, and lit the touchpaper.

While I retreated like my life depended on it, the rocket took off with that long scraping sound they make, like sandpaper being rubbed quickly over a length of wood. High above the silhouettes of the houses, a shower of brilliant green and blue stars cascaded back towards the ground as the gunpowder detonated. In Jana's back garden, there were a few seconds of complete, beautiful silence. At that moment, no cars, no sirens, no voices, just wonderful empty bluey-blackness. And, with the rocket, a few of my worries exploded too. For the first time in the weekend, I had a glimmer things might be all right. Don't know why.

'God hears all our prayers,' Jana said softly. 'And answers them in his own way. Time to go home!'

And then, of course, I found I was crying again. Good thing no one could see.

I was last out of the door as everyone left, wrapping up in coats and scarves, being collected by parental chauffeurs.

'Want to hang around and tell me about it? We can walk you home later.' Jana said surreptitiously among the goodbyes.

I nodded.

An hour later, when I'd cracked completely under interrogation, Jana had the headlines of everything that had happened since September.

'Goodness!' she said. 'Well, that's about enough to be going on with, isn't it?'

She thought for a few seconds, and while I waited, the sounds of Jana's house became very loud: little creaks, a clock, a breeze tugging at the windows.

Jana went very serious on me. 'Look,' she said, 'I spend a lot of my time letting clients find their own way through things, allowing *them* to get a grip on what they think and want. But for your own preservation, Abi, I'm going to *tell* you what to do. You've got to get your priorities straight. You've probably got to make a list of the most important things and people, and concentrate on them. If it means you have to drop some things, then I think maybe you just have to. Whatever they are. Even Tomorrow's People if that seems right!'

Did she mean it? She didn't. I know she didn't. I could hear from the tone of voice that in her opinion, Tomorrow's People should come somewhere near the top of the list of priorities. In a way, Jana was like everyone else. Just slightly more subtle with it. I tried to butt in with a, 'Yeah, but...'

Jana wouldn't let me.

'Hang on a second, Abi. Though it's hard for you, I think you've got to accept you can't say "yes" to everyone. And I think you've got to face up to the consequences of doing that. But I promise, people will still like you, and want to be with you, because there's a great deal about *you* to like…'

I looked sceptical.

'Really! It's just that no one, not you, not me, can fix everybody and everything! All you can do is pray for them. Let God do some work, for heaven's sake. It's not all down to you!'

'I can't fix anything at all,' I said, suddenly stressed out all over again. 'What about Mum and Dad?'

'Talk to them. Or give them a chance to talk to you. And try not to let your imagination run away with you!'

So, later on, just before I banged my head on the pillow five times, I decided Jana was right in at least one respect. I had to go back on what I'd said and tell AD with all the politeness I could muster that his concert idea was totally naff, and I *really* couldn't take it on. Not this term, anyway.

But back in school on Monday, AD was nowhere to be found. Or Zoe Hughes. Same on Tuesday. On a course, someone said. Ill, someone else thought. But since Wednesday after-school was the appointed time for Jana's A Club meditation workshop, and AD was bound to be there then, I thought to myself, *OK, it can wait till then.*

Wednesday lunchtime, as I was going down to Brookfield for afternoon school, my gob was fairly smacked to see Tyler Dunn tucked into a grubby little corner near the main Willowmede gates. He deliberately blanked me, turning his back with a go-away-little-girl sneer. Like I should care anyway! But beside him, chatting away nineteen to the dozen, was a girl in standard customized Willowmede uniform: skirt hitched way up, white t-shirt showing beneath polo shirt, plus definitely non-regulation, dangly, confiscate-me-if-you-dare earrings. She didn't see me.

Blimey!, I thought. *Char!*

A telltale little funnel of blue-grey smoke rose into the air from invisible cigarettes being held at waist height. At least, I suppose the smoke was from regular cigarettes. Me, I wouldn't know the difference, would I? Might have been the other thing.

If I thought about it, Char *had* been undergoing a bit of a makeover in the last week or so. She'd been pushing the Willowmede rules, wearing a bit more slap. She even looked a bit slimmer, a bit more grown-up, though apart from the lipgloss, I'm not sure I can tell you exactly *how*. And maybe, come to mention it, a whiff of tobacco had been following her around.

I nailed her after school, by the lockers, just before the meditation session.

'What are you *doing*?' I said, jumping in with both feet. So much for my new resolution about not trying to fix everybody and everything! That had lasted all of two days.

Char didn't get what I was on about, though she could see I was het up.

'What?'

'Tyler Dunn!'

'So?'

'I saw you. At lunchtime. Sharing a puff with Tyler.'

Char didn't seem particularly put out.

'Yeah?'

'The same Tyler Dunn who beat up Drew the other day!'

'So? Don't jump to conclusions, Abi! And lighten up. Has it crossed your mind I might have been trying to find out why?'

That caused me to stop and think, but I didn't buy it, not really. Tyler and Char had looked like they were enjoying each other's company far too much.

' "Trying to find out why?" You think Tyler needs a reason to be a thug? He's a low life, and that's all you need to know! Go figure, Char! He was probably the one who tried to burn the school down!'

She stared at me; a penetrating, chilly look. There was an echo of her mum in it.

'That's completely outrageous, Abi. You've got absolutely no proof of that. Have you ever *talked* to Tyler?'

Oh no! You don't fancy *him?* I thought. *You don't actually want to get off with Tyler, do you? What is wrong with you, Char?*

'No. He's never exactly offered *me* the chance.'

'Well, if you did, maybe you'd find out a few things. Like, he's very clever…'

'In a criminal sort of way…'

'No, not necessarily in a "criminal sort of way". God, Abi, you are so prejudiced. For one thing, he knows about the A Club, and he's got the hump about it.'

'How come?'

'He thinks we're all up-ourselves, middle class teacher's narks, and Willowmede never does anything for people like him.'

'Middle class teacher's narks like Eddie Finn?'

'I'm not agreeing with Tyler, Abs. I'm telling you what he thinks.'

'So this isn't a regular thing then? You won't be hanging out with him every lunch hour?'

Char's eyes caught fire. I'd hit a nerve.

'None of your business, Abi. I'll spend time with anyone I want to. Might be you. Might be Tyler. Might be the King of Denmark, but it's my life, OK, not yours! And while we're at it, Tyler's got a point. If you ask me, the A Club is all a bit precious, and if it turns people into little clones of you, then my time's best spent elsewhere!'

Char stormed off. That was minus one for meditation then!

Jana had set herself up in the old music room, which doubles as a worship space for Willowmede's Muslims and Catholics. There's a scattering of cushions and a half-decent carpet which hasn't been entirely destroyed by chewing gum. A few days a week the room gets used as a crèche. Big Ben has this idea that babies civilize a school. So I suppose it doesn't do to think what else might have been spilled on there.

Jana had lit the room with candles, which hid the bare patches and Blu-Tack marks on the walls slightly, and she'd brought in a couple of nice old Persian rugs which gave the room a bit more of an exotic aura, and made sitting on the floor slightly more hygienic.

Trouble was, even after waiting ten minutes, there was only AD, Jana, Drew, Sally and me. *Now the A Club is collapsing,* I thought gloomily. And it was partly my fault, falling out first with Em and now Char. The ratfink AD certainly looked a bit concerned about the turnout. There was no Hughesey to hold his hand either.

Jana gave us some breathing routines, and then did some focusing exercises using pictures she'd brought with her of old works of art. She played some hypnotic music. She painted some word pictures of beautiful places and situations. And we talked for a little while about how we thought meditation could help us study better. Her theme was 'Rhythms of Life' – how there are going to be ups and downs every week. Like, tell me about it! But it was all very nice and relaxing. Then, at the end, she asked us if we'd share one bad thing and one good thing about the day. Being a meanie, she picked on me first.

'Falling out with a friend. Again!' I scowled, thinking to myself that the normal Char might have enjoyed all this hippie stuff. Then, playing it for laughs, I added. 'But at least it didn't rain.'

'Maths test,' said Drew, 'and your session!'

Creep!

'Me next,' said Jana. 'My car failed its MOT. It cost me a lot of money. But, and this was amazingly wonderful, I saw a lesser spotted woodpecker in my back garden. I've never seen one before. What about you, Sally?'

Sally seemed stuck to find anything bad. 'But the good news is my Dad says he's going to be at home all Christmas,' she said triumphantly. 'Which he hasn't been since I can't remember when.'

'What about you, Dr Dickson?' asked Jana.

AD jumped when he heard his name, like he'd been miles away, or as if, because he was the teacher, he thought he wouldn't have to make a contribution. He looked completely stumped. He spread his hands, shook his head slowly and swallowed hard. I could see Jana suddenly realizing she'd hit a sore spot. Of course AD wasn't going to share anything personal in front of us. She backed off, adding hurriedly, 'Of course, only if you want to…'

'No, no,' he said. 'It's funny. I just can't think of anything. Isn't that silly! Don't mind me…'

I knew how he felt. Remember, I'd been there just a few days before, suddenly put on the spot. And looking at him, I had the strongest feeling that, like me, there was something AD really wanted to say, but didn't dare. Not in present company. I wondered what it was. Something good? No. It had to be something really bad, didn't it?

What more can I say? I suppose I could try to kid you it was the alien's fault, but the fact is, I just lost my nerve. I chickened out of telling AD where he could put his concert, by convincing myself it wasn't a good moment. Aren't I a softie?

Afterwards, I helped Jana load up her newly MOT'd moneypit of an old banger with the rugs and stuff, hoping she'd offer me a lift home. Jana was just closing the tailgate, when, with a roar from its twin exhausts, a smart little sports car drew alongside. Rosie Pickings hung her head out of the window, somewhere about the level of our knees.

'Wotcher, Abi,' she said. 'Good A Club?'

'Great,' I said, thinking, *Hasn't she got anything better to do than follow the A Club around? Does she really keep all our dates in her diary? Sad person!*

'Where's your friend Eddie, then?' Rosie asked, peering round the car park and revving her engine, like she was in a hurry to be somewhere else.

'Don't know,' I answered. *What does she want to know that for?* 'Haven't seen him all day.'

'It's Eddie… *Finn*, isn't it?' The way she asked, you could tell she was trying just a little too hard to sound casual about the question.

'Think so!' I said unconvincingly, brain whirring while I thought, *This isn't right. Too much curiosity about someone who should be of absolutely no interest at all.*

'OK,' said Rosie. 'See you around!' And she engaged gear and drove off with a squeal of tyres. If he'd been there, Eddie would have approved.

'Who was *that*?' Jana asked.

'Rosie Pickings,' I said. 'Remember, I told you about her on Sunday. The nosey reporter from the *Examiner*?'

'The face rings a bell,' Jana puzzled. 'But not the name. I'd remember anyone called Pickings, I know I would. It'll probably come back to me. Anyway, come on, let's go home. I need a cup of tea.'

Hmm. Rosie the news hound and Eddie the car thief. It seemed a very bad combination to me.

Just after I'd finished writing up last Sunday's blog, showering and getting ready for church, I was listening to *Motorway FM*'s 'Inspirational Hour'. Ever since the Jessica Taft interview, I've been tuning in occasionally. Yeah, yeah, I know. Not exactly cool. But allow me my Sunday morning brain candy.

They were playing a song which was vaguely familiar. The chorus goes '*What have you done today to make you feel proud?*', several million times over. Heather Small, I think they said, whoever she is. It might be minging by hip Year Nine standards, but it is hooky, and there I was, like you do, gurning around under the shower, well into my own personal karaoke session. Between you and me it's even possible I may have been using my bottle of conditioner as a microphone… '*What have you done today to make you feel…*'

And suddenly I stopped mid-line. The words weren't just words any longer. They meant something.

I put the conditioner/microphone down on the soap tray and stood there in a trance while the shower continued to power water over my goosebumps. Exactly what *had* I done during the last twenty-four hours/week/fortnight/for ever that I could feel truly proud of? It was only too easy to think of stuff which made me look bad and feel ashamed.

Mortified, I turned off the waterfall, pulled on some clothes, and because there were still ten minutes before I needed to leave for St Michael's, scribbled down some thoughts with one hand while I dried my hair with the other. I did what Jana had suggested, and listed my priorities. This is it, as far as you can read it now through the splodges of water and ink.

Abi's Priorities

1. Mum and Dad
a) Find out what's happening.
b) Get used to it, whatever it is. Even if they're going to split. Remember: only five years to uni. Hang on!

2. Friends
a) Make up with Em. Need my best friend back, esp. in view of 1.
b) Make up with Char re: Tyler. Be subtle!
c) Sort Eddie Finn – Rosie Pickings?

3. Who am I?
Dancer or musician? Both or neither? Or something else? Sort it out with Ciarán/Everard. Stop whingeing! Think! What will I be doing in ten years' time, anyway?

4. Knock the A Club on the head!
Does that mean doing AD's show or not? Decide by end of week latest! Stop hesitating!

5. Tomorrow's People?
No! *Yesterday's* people!

I inspected myself in the mirror. Squeezed a spot. Applied a token layer of lippie. And then reread what I'd written. Friends and family. They have to come first, don't they? Would Jana agree?

In church I spent more time looking at my piece of paper, thinking things over, and when I came out I knew what I had to do. The Goodenoughs usually have a family meeting over Monday breakfast, to tell each other what's happening the following week. No point in waiting. Whether Pete was there or not, this Monday I had to raise the Big Question.

Sunday night, I didn't sleep well. Lying there, I kept rehearsing how

I would slide naturally into talking to Mum and Dad about their relationship. What would Jana say? Maybe a leading question. Something like: 'You guys haven't been sounding too happy recently...'

Safe. But they might too easily ignore that, if they wanted to. How about a different angle?

'Char's still really upset about her parents. I don't expect they realize what they've done to her...'

There'd be secret and guilty looks across the breakfast table. But wouldn't that just be rubbing their noses in it? They must already be in pain. It seemed unfair to stress them out even more. What about something to make them feel better?

'Do you think parents should always stay together for the sake of the children? Well, I don't! If it were me, I'd much rather...'

Problem was, actually, that was all a load of pants. What I really wanted to say was, 'You dirty rats. Don't you understand you're messing me up? Get a grip!'

How about hitting it head-on? 'Are you two thinking of getting a divorce?'

But I couldn't see myself really asking that either.

As I tossed and turned, I kept looking at the alarm clock. I know I saw it say one o'clock, two fifteen and ten past three, but then I must have fallen more deeply asleep, because the next thing I remember it was just after five, and oddly, even before I was really awake, I could distinctly hear this strange, *wrong* noise underneath me and downstairs, as if someone was pulling the table across the floor. Then there was a double cough. A wheezing, asthmatic, smoker's cough. Not a Goodenough cough. Hang on, hadn't we been here before? Surely history couldn't be repeating itself? Except this time I knew for certain there were no sleepwalking guests in the house.

I threw myself out of bed and, making as much racket as I could, I bundled out of the bedroom, bouncing off the furniture as I went, stamping on the floor, banging on Mum and Dad's door, turning on lights and trying to make whoever was in our house think there were a dozen very large Goodenoughs all coming to get him.

Dad clattered out of their bedroom, pumped up with adrenalin, followed by a pale and shocked-looking Mum. Pete stuck a tousled, confused head out of his door. Dad had a walking stick in his hand.

'I'm armed,' he shouted improbably down the staircase at the possible intruder.

I suppose this was technically true, but if you knew my dad, you'd immediately see just how absurd it was. In the family photograph album there are pictures of him when he was younger, on peace marches and stuff with a beard and badges, and he doesn't like most modern sports because they're 'too violent'. In short, and in the nicest possible way, my dad's a bit of a wuss.

When we got downstairs, the kitchen door was swinging open. It looked like whoever had been there had legged it. We must have missed them by seconds. Dad clapped a hand to his forehead. 'I'm sure I locked that door before I came up,' he said, though it was obvious from his guilty reaction he knew he hadn't. He turned to Pete and me and said accusingly, 'Did either of you go out last night?'

'No,' grunted a very surly Pete. 'Why would I want to go in your cruddy back garden?'

This rang completely true. Pete couldn't find his way to the rubbish heap. I shouldn't think he's been on our lawn since he was about ten, when it became too small for his games of footie.

'My laptop,' Mum suddenly exclaimed. 'It was on the table. It's gone. And my mobile. *And* my car keys.'

And at that moment we all heard the sound of Mum's beloved Ford Ka being revved to the max and screeching out of the Goodenough driveway at a hundred and fifty miles an hour.

'Oh, Dave…' she said, looking reproachfully at Dad, who for a moment was an open-mouthed, pajama-wearing statue. Mum collapsed backwards into a chair, just about as defeated as I've ever seen her.

'Well, *do* something, Dave!' she said after a few seconds, waving her balled fists at him, like it was nothing to do with her. Dad was still rooted to the spot, catatonic with his own stupidity in leaving the back door unlocked.

All there *was* to do was ring the police, who turned up with a polite knock at the door around quarter to six. The two cops were very kind, and we all drank several cups of tea while they took down our story about five times on ten different forms. Then there was a call on the police radio to say Mum's car had been found two miles away, smashed into a bollard down the dual carriageway.

And so deep gloom descended on the House of Goodenough. Pete went back to bed. I wandered aimlessly round the house, my legs suddenly jelly-like, trying to think straight. Shock, I suppose.

'Do you want me to write a note for school, love?' Mum asked, seeing me drifting about, so braindead.

'What does she need a note for?' Dad snapped. 'It's done and dusted. Abi's got to get on with life. Like the rest of us. No point in making a drama out of a crisis.'

'That's fine for you to say,' said Mum, rising to the bait. 'It's not *your* computer that's been stolen is it? Or *your* car that's been trashed? All because someone forgot to lock the back door?'

'Oh, I see!' Dad said huffily. 'I thought we were talking about Abi. Not you!'

'Excuse me?' I interrupted. 'Can anyone join in? Thanks, Mum, but no thanks. I'll be OK without a note. And actually, can I just say it won't help if we all start biting each other's heads off?'

They both looked a bit shamefaced, but the way things were, I was fairly sure they'd have another go when I was safely out of the way.

So much for priorities! So much for me finding out if a divorce was on the cards! That too would have to wait now, at least for a few days.

Truthfully, I wasn't really on the case most of Monday morning. My mind kept wandering off and running pointless action replays of the robbery, like seeing a goal going in from fifteen million different angles on telly. Penny caught me looking mindlessly out of the window at the building site and was his usual charming self.

'I had heard rumours my lessons were as exciting as watching paint dry, Abigail, but there's no need to make it so devastatingly obvious...'

Funny way to get yourself an A level student! Penny's sense of humour is so posh, it scarcely raised a titter. The man is a complete moron.

It takes me about twenty-one minutes flat out (half walk, half unladylike sprint) to get from Willowmede to my front door, so I thought to myself that if anyone else was at home, that's where I wanted to be during Monday's longer lunchtime, even if only for twenty minutes. I phoned Dad at break, and he said he'd be in. Mum was going to be at the prison. There'd been an emergency call because a prisoner had escaped, and she had to be there to make sure he didn't get beaten up when they finally caught him. By the prison officers, not the other cons!

'You don't have to come home,' he added.

'I know I don't,' I replied. 'But I want to!'

When I'd panted in through the front door he was already boiling a kettle.

'I feel such an idiot!' he said and shook his head sadly. 'What a senior moment! I always check that door. How come I didn't do it last night?'

'Could have happened to anyone,' I said and hugged him, though I caught myself thinking, *Yes, it can! But do grown-ups cut us kids slack when we forget stuff? I don't think so!*

'Is everything OK with you and Mum now?' I asked, trying to make the question sound casual as I searched the fridge for anything which might make a half-decent sandwich.

Dad looked sharply at me.

'Yeah. She'll be fine. We'll get the money back on the insurance for the computer and the car. By the sound of it, your mum's been sensible, so everything of importance on the laptop was backed up. Oh, and I've been out to take a look at the car this morning. They can repair the damage. It's more inconvenience than anything else. They'll even give your mum a hire car while her own's being fixed.'

'And the two of you are really all right?'

145

He laughed it off, but the laugh didn't sound convincing to me.

'Yeah, you know how it is. Storm in a teacup.'

'Lot of teacups recently…'

'No! Have there been? No more than normal, surely?'

And he looked keenly at me again, as if trying to fathom what was going on inside my head. We were playing a game, and we both knew it, but I was running out of time. School beckoned, and that was as far as I was going to get just then.

As I dashed back up the road leading to Willowmede, checking my watch obsessively to make sure I beat the bell, Tyler Dunn was slouching along the other way, off on the wag. From a hundred metres apart it was obvious neither of us could avoid passing the other. Even so, I crossed over so we didn't have to share the same pavement.

As we drew parallel with each other, he did something odd. He smiled broadly (I nearly said 'evilly'), licked his finger, and made a 'one-up' sign in the air. Instantly I joined up his gesture with the burglary. How could Tyler have heard about the break-in already so soon? Char would be the most likely source. But Drew was the only one I'd had a chance to tell. Maybe Drew had told Char. Or was it conceivably possible Tyler knew *because he'd been there*? He couldn't really be that much of a crim? Could he?

After Sunday's all-nighter, I slept so heavily that Mum had to shake me awake on Tuesday morning. I hadn't heard the alarm at all. And for once the knocking-my-head-on-the-pillow trick hadn't worked either. On my bleary-eyed way down to Willowmede, I decided that if number one on my list of priorities wasn't negotiable at present, at least I could tackle number two. So should it be Em or Char first?

Char was sitting on her own in the hall at lunchtime, munching her way through a plastic container's worth of rabbit food, looking like she was hating every mouthful. Still, that's probably how she was losing the pounds. Ever since I'd known her, she'd always been a burger and chips girl. She didn't see me sneaking up on her until it was too late. I plonked myself down, looked her right in the eyes, and said as sincerely as I knew how, 'Char, I'm really sorry!'

'What for?' she said, scooping wayward bits of cress off her chin.

'For telling you your business.'

She swallowed, and cleared her throat.

'Yeah, well, you were out of order. But I forgive you. It's no big deal. Tyler's a jerk. But he might be a useful jerk. And if you get to know him, there's more to him than being a thug. Really there is!'

'If you say so.'

'I do. He's made some bad friends, and he knows it, but he's working hard at putting distance between himself and them.'

'He tells you this?'

'Yeah! But c'mon, Abs, you can't go round disbelieving everything everybody says, can you?'

'OK. But it's been a really lousy week so far...'

'I heard about the break-in. From Drew...'

Of course, I was curious to know whether Char was the source of Tyler's apparent knowledge about the burglary, but in the interests of peace it seemed like that should wait or be forgotten entirely. Instead, I turned the conversation round to Rosie Pickings' curiosity about Eddie.

'That woman is a total pain in the bum,' raged Char. 'She's been snooping about round Thornton Bramleigh too.'

'Never...'

'Oh yes! We caught her cruising up and down the village street last Saturday morning. Watching for comings and goings at our house, I expect. All the reporters from the national papers gave up and went home yonks ago, but not her. Trying to make a name for herself, Mum says. I even saw her parked outside AD's house the other evening, poking her nose in. She's obsessed with Willowmede, I reckon.'

'Digging for dirt? That's awful!'

An image of AD and Hughesey much in love and driving us back from London in the minibus suddenly shot into my mind. Pompous idiot though AD is, the two of them didn't deserve to have Rosie Pickings snooping into their lives. What they got up to at home was their own private business and no one else's.

'Seems like it. And that's the last thing they need at the moment, I should think.'

I seemed to be missing something here.

'What do you mean?'

'Didn't I say?'

'Say what?'

'Oh! Well, it's a bit sad really. Mum got it from the woman who works in the village post office. Hughesey's got a bad cancer scare. Found a lump. Sounds like it might be serious. Hospital and stuff.'

The things Char knows. She's definitely got a future as a gossip columnist. Suddenly I thought of the way AD had been at Jana's meditation session. Was *that* what had been on his mind? I turned my feelings back into fury with Rosie.

'How can Rosie Pickings live with herself? Spending her entire time making other people's lives a misery. What have you or AD or Eddie ever done to her?'

'It's what they do. They're just rats, Abi. All journalists are sewer rats. They can't help themselves.'

'Well,' I said, so relieved that in the face of a common enemy Char was talking to me again, 'maybe the first thing *we* should do is put the wind up Eddie, and see if we can't keep him out of mischief. Neutralize him. At least remove *him* from Rosie's clutches.'

'Don't fancy our chances. Once a twocer, always a twocer...'

'Twocer?'

'Taking a vehicle without consent. It's what they call it.'

'So there's no hope for Eddie, but you'd give Tyler a second chance?'

I had to get *that* dig in! At least Char had the grace to smile.

'OK, look! I'll support your good cause, if you'll help me with my mine. Deal?'

We shook on it, but I still didn't feel Tyler Dunn and I were ever likely to become bosom buddies.

Em was a harder nut to crack. It seemed like I followed her around most of Wednesday, trying to keep up, and make a space to apologize for whatever it was I was supposed to have done wrong. Finally I trapped her in a corner and began, 'Look, Em, you and me... We're still friends, aren't we?'

'If you like.'

'What does that mean? Are we or aren't we?'

'Whatever!'

'No. Not whatever. It matters to me, Em. It really does. If you just prefer other people, or it doesn't matter to you, then tell me, and that's fine. Well... it's not fine, but it'll have to do. But at the moment I don't understand why you're in such a strop with me. If I've got things wrong, I'm sorry, but I hate it being like this...'

Em turned and glared.

'Maybe you just hate not being the centre of attention all the time, Abi. Maybe that's what you hate...'

'I know,' I said wretchedly, 'I know. I do like the limelight. You're quite right. I like making things happen. And sometimes it gets out of hand. I found it really hard that you got to be basketball captain. But I'm working on it, I promise. And Em, right now I need your help! Not for me. For someone else. Something important.'

I suppose I hoped asking for help would press Em's buttons, and I was right. It did. She softened visibly. I explained about Rosie's possible attempt to get at Eddie, and what Char had told me about Zoe Hughes.

'So what we need to do,' I finished, 'and I mean all of us together – is to make Eddie see how absolutely squeaky clean he needs to be at the moment – not just for him, but for AD and Hughesey too. They don't need anything else to worry about. The way I see it, we can't give Rosie a centimetre to get at the A Club or Willowmede! And honest, Em, this isn't me wanting to be the centre of attention. I'm just trying to make things the best they can be! Once we've cracked December, I'll give up completely and let everyone do what they want!'

'Oh, go on then,' Em muttered. 'Where do we form the posse?'

Early doors on Thursday morning, we pieced together where Eddie would be during the day, and between us mounted an Eddie-watch. We drew a blank at lunchtime. He seemed to have vanished off the face of the earth. But at the end of afternoon school, Char, Em, Drew and I found him near the teachers' car park, looking wistfully through the railings at its contents.

'Eddie?' Em called quietly from behind him. Even so, it was enough to make him jump.

'We want to talk to you,' said Drew menacingly. It sounded like a line from a gangster movie.

'Yeah? What about?' Eddie's eyes lingered lustfully for a few seconds over Miss Watkinson's new bright blue Peugeot coupé, which lay a few tantalizing metres away on the other side of the fence, then reluctantly and slightly sulkily focused back on us.

'You would, wouldn't you!' Char said, picking up on Eddie's train of thought. 'You'd be up the road in the Wazzo-Wagon if you got half a chance!'

'Do us a favour! Who do you think I am?' Eddie sounded indignant. 'It's only a puny Peugeot, innit?' He clicked his teeth. 'Painted and polished tin can, that's what it is!'

'Eddie,' I said, 'you've got to stop. You've *really* got to stop.'

'I wasn't doin' nothing, was I?' he protested. 'Just looking!'

We explained in words of one syllable. We cajoled. (I like that word!) We walked and talked. Eddie, under our pressure, almost had a case of verbal diarrhoea. He said more consecutive words that I've ever heard him say. Zoe Hughes' possible problem seemed to strike a chord.

'Me auntie died from one of them,' he remarked morosely. 'Didn't get it seen to, me mam said. Shame!'

He was pretty upfront about the twocing too.

'Don't know why I do it, really. Can't help myself. Sometimes just get the urge, d'you know what I mean?'

We nodded, which didn't mean we did.

'I just see something I fancy and... vroom!... way to go! I suppose it's the power 'n' stuff. Feels good while I'm doing it. Then

150

I don't need to nick anything no more. Not for a while... They've had me in court a couple of times...'

'Does anyone at school know?'

'Yeah!' Eddie sounded almost proud. 'AD. And Big Ben. AD's been to court with me, 'cos me mam and dad wouldn't come.'

'What about Rosie Pickings? Does she know?'

'That newspaper woman? Maybe. Not very good at her job if she don't. But what can *she* do? She can't say my name in the paper, can she. I'm only fourteen, innit?'

Em towered over Eddie, her hunched shoulders and narrow features like a human vulture. 'Listen to me, Eddie, you've got to stop being so selfish! It's not just your life, is it? If you end up in court again, Rosie can make a connection with Willowmede and the A Club. She doesn't have to say much to diss the whole thing, and make us all look like the scroats she believes inhabit this place!'

Eddie looked thoughtful.

'I want to give it a go,' he said. 'I know I can't go on nickin', or I'm gonna end up inside, like me brother Dom. But what do I do when I get the urge?' He spread his hands hopelessly.

'We'll help,' I chipped in. 'You know... accentuate the positive. Concentrate on one hour at a time, and think about how you can make it something to be proud of!'

Mary Poppins and Heather Small crossed with Jana. Yuk!

'You can do it,' said Em encouragingly. 'I know you can. Come and find one of us whenever you think you might be getting the urge...'

And I remembered why Em was my best friend. She can be a pillock, but she can also be a very nice person.

An uncomfortable thought flitted through my mind. Just for a couple of seconds. Did Eddie ever get urges in the middle of the night? Housebreaking wasn't among his other achievements, was it? It was an unworthy thought, and I pushed it away.

Jana called on Friday evening.

'I've had an idea,' she said. 'About your friend, Rosie Pickings.

When I'd just started as a magistrate, maybe ten years ago, I remember there was a case involving Willowmede and a girl called Rosie. Her name wasn't Pickings though, I'm sure of that. But this Rosie's face makes me think there might be a connection. Thought you might like to know. Could be worth checking out, if she's being a pain!'

'How do we do that?' I asked.

'Well, ironically, the *Examiner*'s own records may show it. Or they may keep old copies of the paper on microfiche at the local library. You just ring up and ask. If I'm not getting muddled, it was late March one year. There was a sudden heavy snowfall which caught everybody on the hop.'

'If I can find anything on her, how's it going to help?' I said.

'Well,' chuckled Jana, 'there's a bit in the Bible which tells us to be "cunning as a serpent". Maybe you need to find your snakey side, Abi!'

I wasn't sure I understood what Jana meant.

Blog the Thirteenth
4 December

Sunday afternoon at the Goodenoughs. Dad out in the garden, chasing the fading light and sweeping up the leaves which have blown in from next door onto our lawn. Ban all immigrant leaves! Pete upstairs in his room playing his guitar (!) and singing (!!), which is very strange and wonderful because Pete a) knows only three chords at most and b) had never sung in his life before until a fortnight ago. But now he's formed a band with some other blokes from college, like the world needs any more talentless rock'n'roll bands. They're called *Adrenalin Rush*, though from the noise Pete's making, the only rush they're going to give anyone is to the vomit bowl.

Mum, Hannah and I in the sitting room. Hannah *knitting* because someone's told her it's the trendy thing to do. Mum and I have avoided asking her what it's going to be, but it's pink and white and expanding in unpredictable directions. Mum reading something about prisons, and me doing maths homework which I only 10% understand. The telly is on: old episodes of *The Bill* on a satellite channel. Hannah's deeply into it, bug-eyed and dropping stitches by the dozen. Occasionally I get distracted from equations and sets, watching out of the corner of one eye. It suddenly comes to me that *The Bill*'s plots only work because there's an unspoken scriptwriters' rule that no character ever tells any other character anything if it's a matter of importance. Zero communication. (Except there's a second rule too: if anyone ever says to someone, 'You mustn't tell anyone about this…', they must instantly run off and tell everyone in sight!)

Suddenly it clicks with me that if the A Clubbers are to survive the term in one piece, keeping everyone in the loop 100% of the time is a must. I head for the computer, and immediately wish I hadn't, because now Pete's singing is all too clearly audible. He's moaning like a cow on the toilet. And I think to myself that if this is going to be more than a two-week wonder, I'm going to have to buy earplugs. Just a typical Sunday afternoon at Goodenough Towers.

There and then I emailed everyone a) to tell them Jana's hunch about Rosie Pickings and ask if anyone fancied coming down the library with me after school on Monday to check it out and b) to suggest we really had to meet asap to finally deal with AD's concert thing. I grovelled mightily and said how the situation was now desperate and it had to be all hands to the pump. Yes, well, I've finally decided. Let's do it and not rock AD's boat for now. Then see where we are with the A Club in January. Am I weakening? No. Adapting.

Drew and Em volunteered for the library. And all seven major league A Clubbers agreed to meet at Sally's on Wednesday evening for the concert-planning. We'd make it a sort of party because it had to be fun for us too. At least there was the bonus I'd get to visit the Kennedy pad at last and see how the other half live.

The librarian looked suspicious when the three of us pitched up at her enquiry desk, like we were a riot waiting to happen. She made a hushed phone call. In a few minutes a small furry animal minion appeared noiselessly beside us, squinting furiously. Why are the people who work in the Castilian Street library such weirdos? There's not one that doesn't have a wooden leg or the shakes.

'Elspeth will show you what to do,' the librarian whispered fiercely. Or hoarsely. Perhaps she just had a bad throat.

Elspeth, the furry minion, led us into a side room with tables mostly occupied by elderly men in tweed jackets reading books the size of small forests. Down one side of the room were a row of VDUs. Elspeth squinted into one of them. She hit a few buttons, twiddled a few knobs and tutted a million times before finally saying triumphantly, 'There you are!'

She showed us how to scroll backwards and forwards through the

Examiner's archives, and left us to it, while she pitter-pattered back to her burrow. The tweed jackets looked at us severely over their half-moon glasses, waiting for the chance to have us thrown out.

Drew grabbed the controls and scrolled madly backwards. Suddenly we were in 1975 and reading the gory details of a train crash just outside Leicester. Twenty-three people killed. Now I understood the Elspeth squint. The microfiche print was very small.

'I've heard about that,' whispered Em. 'My uncle was an ambulance driver. He was called to the scene.'

'Let's see. I wonder if there's anything about Leicester City?' mused Drew, zeroing in unerringly on some sports pages from 1983, fine-tuning his scrolling technique.

'It's like a time machine,' said Em, suddenly stunned by the awesome power under Drew's fingers.

'Guys,' I said. 'All very fascinating, but…'

Reluctantly, Drew time travelled away from 1983 and found the March of ten years ago.

'Look for anything which mentions "snow chaos",' I said. 'According to Jana, that's likely to be the big story of the day in question.'

But there was no mention of snow that March. The *Examiner*'s a daily evening paper, so we were speed-checking a lot of newsprint.

'It's a needle in a haystack job,' said Drew, leaning back. 'Take your pick. Do we try March of the years either side, or April and February of the same year?'

'Or is there an index?' asked Em sensibly.

'Nice one,' I said. 'Let's see if Elspeth knows.'

So we summoned Elspeth again, but no, there wasn't an index. So it was back to guesswork.

'Follow the March thing,' I said. 'I reckon Jana's probably good on that sort of detail.'

So we tried a year later, and then we tried a year earlier, and then, bingo! On 27 March there was a report of six inches of snow falling late one afternoon, 'paralysing Leicester'.

'Got to be it,' I said. Drew was whizzing around on the scroll bar. 'Slowly, slowly! It might be a very small article.'

But actually it wasn't. There was a picture too.

'That's her!' exclaimed Em loudly. *Very* loudly! The tweed suits cleared their throats.

'Sorry,' she whispered, turning and smiling sweetly at them. Honestly, we tried not to giggle.

'It is, though. Look!'

Certainly the face was the same, though this was a younger Rosie. She had shoulder length hair, and was wearing a trouser suit probably meant to make her look intelligent and honest for the court. It was just a size or so too large, and hung off her rather slim frame awkwardly.

'What does it say?'

We peered at the screen.

'At Leicester Crown Court today, twenty-year-old Ann-Rosemarie Sanders was given a three month suspended jail sentence following a guilty verdict in the Willowmede School hate-mail case. The court was told that Miss Sanders, a former pupil, believed the school to be responsible for her examination failure and subsequently exacted revenge by a sustained series of threats and slanderous accusations. In one case, a member of staff was so upset that she was said to have made a suicide attempt. Sentencing Sanders, Recorder Andrew Openshaw said, "By your reprehensible actions you have caused great distress to staff and students. It is only by virtue of your previous good character and considerable personal potential that you do not find yourself beginning a prison sentence. You should be under no illusion that a repetition of this behaviour will have grave consequences." '

'Blimey!' said Em. 'Who'd want to be called Ann-Rosemarie?'

'Wouldn't that make her too old, though?' Drew was sceptical. 'And what about the Sanders thing?'

'Rosie could easily be thirty,' I said. 'It's hard to tell how old people are just from looking at them. And as for being called Sanders, how do we know she isn't married, or has been? Maybe she's simply changed her name. Or uses "Pickings" as a professional name. I've always thought that was a bit too obvious for a reporter. Far too much of a pun.'

'So what does a "suspended sentence" mean, then?' asked Em. 'Did she go to prison or didn't she?'

'Means if she did it again, it was, "go to jail, do not pass go, do not collect two hundred quid!" ' said Drew.

'Sssh!' The tweed suits tapped their fingers impatiently on the tables.

'What this shows is that she *does* have a grudge against Willowmede!' I hissed. I looked around. 'Where's Elspeth? Let's see if we can get a copy of this.'

We paid our pound, and took away the single copy of the article we were allowed. Outside the library, we agreed not to divulge the contents to anyone beyond the inner circle of the A Club for the time being.

'What are we going to do, now we know?' asked Drew.

'Wait and see what happens,' I said. 'Don't you think?'

In fact, we only had to wait until the next day.

Em and I were trailing out of assembly on Tuesday morning when AD stopped us.

'Got a moment?' he said, like we could choose whether we went to double Biology or not.

AD's eyes were roving all around the Willowmede hall. His left hand was playing absent-mindedly with the keys of a palmtop. We had about a quarter of his attention, if we were lucky.

'If that's chewing gum, Reivers,' he said, raising his voice to a passing, scowling Year Nine chav more commonly answering to the name of Rip on account of an unpleasant habit of polluting the environment with his own patented and peculiarly disgusting range of smells, 'find a bin and leave it there.' AD's voice dropped again. Almost under his breath he said, 'How's the concert going?'

'Everything's under control,' I answered evasively.

'Good, good…' he said. On the far side of the hall Hughesey was walking slowly towards a door, huddling herself up in a cardigan. I don't know if it was my imagination, but she seemed a thin, forlorn figure.

'So all the talent's primed and ready to go, is it?' AD murmured distractedly.

'More or less,' I lied. 'We're meeting on Wednesday to finalize the details.'

'Good, good...' muttered AD, finally focusing and turning his attention to us. 'Sorry... What were you saying?'

'We're meeting on Wednesday to sort it out,' I said a second time, speaking that little bit louder and slower as if AD were an OAP or a foreigner. 'You don't want to come, do you, sir?'

It slipped out without my meaning it, and I didn't need Em's dig in the ribs to instantly regret my invitation. Bother! We held our breath.

'No... No.' For a moment there, AD was definitely considering it as a possibility. 'Just tell me what you've decided. By the end of the week?'

He was about to pull away, and allow us to go and celebrate the mysteries of human reproduction, when he had a second thought.

'I had a call from Rosie Pickings yesterday afternoon,' he muttered thoughtfully. 'Says she wants to come and see me on Thursday about the A Club. That it's important and I really ought to make the time. Very odd – just didn't sound right to me. There's nothing I should know, is there?'

'No, sir,' I said, all wide-eyed innocence. 'Haven't a clue!'

I tried not to look at Em. Was this the moment to tell AD that Rosie might have been spying on him and Hughesey? Or that she might have stuff on Eddie and knew about the Ellison family scandal? No! If we had the opportunity to head Rosie off at the pass, we should take it. Nothing would be gained now by spooking AD that even his relationship with Hughesey might be under the spotlight.

'Well, it's probably something and nothing. But if you do get wind of anything out of the ordinary, you'll let me know, won't you?'

His eyes lingered on us suspiciously, and then he snapped back into business mode. 'You'd better get to your lessons. Tell whoever's teaching you it's my fault for keeping you, won't you?'

'What do we do now?' asked Em, as we ran up the steps of the Biology lab.

'Obvious, isn't it?' I said. 'We've got to get to Rosie first, haven't we? And face her with her past.'

'But that would be...'

'Yup. Blackmail. More or less.'

Did blackmail count as 'the cunning of a serpent'?

'We've got some interesting information about Willowmede for you...' I said into the phone. Slight extra weight on the word 'interesting'. Trying to reel her in.

'Oh?' Rosie Pickings, or Ann-Rosemarie Sanders, or whatever her real name was, sounded curious. 'What sort of information, exactly?'

'It's a bit difficult just now,' I said, looking at the others. 'What about after school today. In Café Doppio?' I looked at Em and Drew for agreement. They nodded. 'About five o'clock?'

A meet was agreed.

All seven A Clubbers had decided it should be Drew, Em and me doing the business. Three of us, because that seemed a reasonable match for Rosie. Not Char or Eddie because of their potential news interest. And Syl and Sally seemed perfectly happy not to be involved in the face-off.

I don't know about the other two, but I was dead nervous as we caught the bus down into town after school.

'Let's do it right,' Drew had said, 'and be professional about this. We don't want to get out-psyched here. Dump your bags at my place. Let's put the photocopy from the microfiche in a folder, and look as smart as we can.'

'You what?' Em exploded. 'That's marvellous coming from you!'

Well, it's true, Drew's usually the one with the permanent bad hair day and inky fingers. But we took his point, and freshened up at his house, so we did look pretty organized and impressive when we pitched up at Café Doppio.

Rosie was already at a table, looking at her watch. We were five minutes late, and probably only just in time. From her impatient vibe, I reckon she'd have legged it if we'd been a second or two longer.

'Hi guys,' she said, and then, cutting straight to the chase, 'what have you got for me?'

'Do you mind if we just get a coffee first?' asked Drew. Perhaps the A Club thing was working for Drew at least. He seemed so much more confident than a month ago. He was good at this, very cool and collected. His request seemed to throw Rosie off beam.

'Yes. Yes, of course. Sorry, I'm just a bit tight on time, that's all.'

'Do *you* want anything?'

'No. No, thanks!'

'Won't be a sec,' we said and disappeared together up to the counter for two of Doppio's cappuccinos and a latte.

'So…' she said, when we'd returned with the drinks and settled ourselves down.

Very deliberately, Drew extracted one of the photocopies from the folder, and slid it slowly across the table towards Rosie. She glanced at it for no more than a second, looked away briefly and then down at her clasped hands. The muscles around her neck and jaw went tense. The colour seeped away from her face.

The café clattered around us, but no one was saying anything around our table. Em and I exchanged eye-contact. Rosie's jaw clenched and unclenched. Her breathing was quick and shallow. She reached for her handbag and drew out a Ventolin inhaler, fingering it nervously. I wouldn't have guessed she was an asthmatic.

'What we think,' said Em, 'is that everyone makes mistakes in their lives. Might be people who have affairs. Or kids who can't help stealing cars. Or teachers. Or… reporters?' She paused for effect. 'And we also think that raking over stuff just for the sake of giving people a thrill isn't on. There's a time for forgetting, and moving on.

160

Do you see what we mean?'

Rosie didn't move a muscle. Her gaze alternated between the ghost which had materialized on the table in front of her and the Ventolin inhaler which twisted and turned between her blood-red fingernails.

'And we don't think,' I added, in case Em hadn't made it sufficiently clear, 'that you're the kind of person who'd want to damage *us* or our friends, just because *you* had a bad time at Willowmede. Are you?'

That was a bit of a stretch, because of course that was exactly what Rosie *was* doing.

'Yes,' she said finally and slowly. 'All very clever of you. Clearly, the three of you have great futures in investigative journalism. Probably better than mine. So well done you. And, yes! Yes, I get your drift.'

'So let's be clear about it then ,' said Drew. The boy's definitely going to be a lawyer. If he doesn't turn to big-time crime first. 'The deal's this. Whatever you think you've got on Willowmede, or Dr Dickson, or Miss Hughes, or the A Club, Eddie Finn, the Ellisons, whatever – it gets binned. Once and for all. If you write about the school from now on, it's got to be good stuff. Positive. Helpful.'

'And Ann-Rosemarie Sanders?' Rosie began.

'Who's she?' I said. 'No one I know. Do you, Em? Drew?'

They shook their heads.

'Won't ever be mentioned again,' drawled Drew. 'Not if you keep your side of the bargain.'

'There *is* one other thing,' I said. 'We could do with some help. With a concert. We kind of got landed with it. And now we've got our work cut out to make it happen at all. But it could be a real feel-good story. Young people helping those worse off than themselves. Selfless giving of time and talent. I bet it'll sell papers by the barrowload! Maybe the *Examiner* would like to adopt it… as a community project?'

'You could tell Dr Dickson about your offer… when you see him on Thursday,' added Em.

Rosie grimaced. 'I'll see what I can do,' she said.

We made a dignified exit, leaving Rosie alone in the café. On the pavement outside, Drew punched the air and shouted 'Yes!' And then all of us three serpents slid off to tea and homework. Sssss!

Was I all *that* impressed by the Kennedy pad at Wednesday evening's A Club party/planning meeting? (I keep wanting to call it the Kennedy Space Centre!) Well, not really!

When I was in Year Six I remember there was a fuss on the news about the Queen having plastic tubs for the cornflakes the royal family ate for breakfast each morning. As if just because she was the Queen, the cornflakes should be kept in solid gold caskets or something. I suppose the truth is that even if you're fantastically rich, you've still got to go to the loo and do washing and eat toast. And there's not much you can do to improve on the design of a toilet seat, a washing machine or Hovis, is there? So maybe the Kennedys have bigger or better things than the Goodenoughs (well, they do, actually!) but they're still basically the *same* things.

There was a hassle at home about my going. Stupidly, I let slip to Dad about Bobby Kennedy being a pop star, and immediately he started an 'all pop stars are druggies' panic. Mum weighed in on my side, and off they went on a ding-dong she will/she won't argument with me spectating, which finished with Dad saying, 'Very well then. Fine. If you're happy for your daughter to end up an addict, then let her go.'

And Mum saying, 'Dave, you're being thick-as-a-brick stupid.'

Excellent. Not!

Actually, Dad knew he was out of order, and capitulated with apologies all round on Wednesday morning. Me, I'm getting used to this family row thing, but I *am* going to have to say something soon. OK, I admit it, I chickened out. Again. Yes, I know. Priorities!

If you want the skinny on the Kennedy lifestyle: a) the rooms are pretty big, b) they have lots of sofas and c) Bobby Kennedy's girlfriend Beth has a thing about china cats, which in my opinion is a maximum on the naff scale and spoils the look of the house completely. Beth did a good job of sorting us with biscuits and Coke though. No drug references intended, I mean the drink. Nothing else!

We had a good laugh. And some half-reasonable ideas. Early on we decided that, since I was likely to be singing or dancing or whatnot, Char should be appointed the show's producer, and have the last word on what happened when. Em would be stage manager, because she'd be good at shouting at people on the night and making them behave nicely. Drew and Eddie would look after the lights and sound. Fair enough. But who could we actually con into taking part?

'We should brainstorm,' suggested Drew. 'No idea too daft. Just go for it, and let's work out whether it's doable later.'

So when we'd got through Robbie Williams, and Dick and Dom, and inviting the entire Leicester Tigers rugby club on stage to sing a selection of rugby songs ('No, really,' Char had insisted. 'It's a totally brilliant idea!'), and motorbikes jumping through hoops of fire on stage (Eddie Finn!), we started getting down to the sensible stuff. Plus some oddballs.

'Well, Pete's started a band,' I said foolishly, when we were still brainstorming.

'Great,' Sally enthused. She's a good enthuser. 'What are they called?'

I told her.

'Put them down for a set, then,' she said.

'Are they any good?' Em asked. I shrugged.

'Don't ask me. He's my brother. I'm bound to think he's crap.'

'What about Tyler?' Char piped up.

'What about him?' growled Drew.

'He does this rap thing. With his mates.'

'No way!'

'You said to put anything down, no matter how daft!'

'That's pretty daft.'

'Just write it down, Drew, like you said!'

Reluctantly, Drew obeyed his producer.

At nine fifteen, after a lot of crossing out and argument, and general hilarity (we'd said we could be picked up at nine thirty), Char said, 'Right then, what have we got?'

Drew read out the list.

'Sally's dad, if we can twist his arm, *Adrenalin Rush*...'

Blank looks all round. Well, it's a terrible and instantly forgettable name.

'... Pete Goodenough's band!'

'*If* they really are good enough...'

'Yeah... if they're OK... Abi's spot... plus students from Ciarán's Dance School...'

Char pulled a face.

'Think of the punters they might bring in...' I reminded her.

'... County Youth Choir...'

My turn to make with the sick bag.

'... Same deal, Abs...' Char retorted.

'... Syl and his uncle with their magic acts...'

Syl had been shy about offering this, and at first the idea that he could be any sort of a magician had seemed weird, until Sally had plonked a pack of cards in his hands, and in five minutes we were all convinced. Like I've said before, Syl's a quiet genius! Brain the size of the Spiral Nebula.

'My uncle's got a load of gear,' he'd said. 'You know, sticking-swords-through-people stuff? Boxes that make people disappear. He'd probably help out in a good cause if he's free...'

'So have we got this thing together, then?' Drew asked.

'You've forgotten Tyler,' Char insisted stubbornly. She looked pointedly at me, reminding me of our pact about good causes.

'Tyler,' I said. 'Don't forget Tyler!'

'What do we call it?' said Sally. 'We can't keep calling it "this thing"!'

'SuperShow?' suggested Syl. 'With two capital "S"s.'

At which we all made puking noises and said what a really bad idea. But since we couldn't think of anything better in the last five minutes, 'SuperShow' it stayed.

Em and I found AD on playground duty the next day.

'Sir, we know why Rosie Pickings is coming to see you,' Em chirped.

'Oh, good. So what's the story then?' AD couldn't decide whether to be pleased or nervous.

'She wants to help with SuperShow. Publicity and so on,' I answered.

AD could tell something was wrong, but he didn't know what. He looked very perplexed.

'But why couldn't she just have phoned me?'

We played dumb.

'Really? It sounded more important than that...' he started to say. It was an itch he badly wanted to scratch. Time for route one. Em was just the safe side of rude.

'Sir, just don't go there, all right? Don't ask, and it won't be a problem. Trust us, sir. Do you want us to come along and tell Rosie all about SuperShow?'

'Yeah, sure...' said AD, and sauntered away to break up a scrap on the other side of the playground, still scratching his head.

Blog the Fourteenth
11 December

The post arrived early on Monday morning, and there was a letter for me, the envelope typed and formal-looking. Pete happened to be up early (why?) and had got to the post first, sifting it nosily before anyone else had a chance to look. I thought it was only girls who were supposed to be so into the goss.

'One for Dad, two for Mum. All very boring!' he announced, chucking what looked like bills and bank statements on to the kitchen work surface. 'Ooh, and one for Abs,' he added, holding it out of reach and up to the light for clues as to its origin. He squinted at the typing. 'Not one of your boyfriends, then...'

I snatched the letter off him, having vengefully jabbed my fingers into Pete's ribs hard enough to double him up, and then retired to a corner where no one could look over my shoulder.

Inside was a folded copy of a short piece from the *Examiner*, dated the previous Friday, plus a note from Rosie on a compliments slip.

'Saw this and thought of you!' it read. 'I've sent the same to Eddie at school. Make sure he goes for it, will you!'

Intrigued, I read the article.

'Karting Challenge

'Leicester Raceway in conjunction with Team Leicester Karting today announced their new "Search for Speed" competition. Open to boys and girls aged under sixteen as of 1 January, the competition organizers hope to unearth a new Alonso or Schumacher from the Leicester region. For many world motor racing champions, success in karting has traditionally been the first rung on the ladder to sporting fame. Applicants need to be sponsored by an organization – a school or club – and preferably

to have some previous understanding or involvement in motorsport. The winner will gain a one-year scholarship with Team Leicester and the opportunity to represent them nationally if they show the right stuff.'

I got it. This was the new, responsible Rosie, letting us know she'd heard what we'd said the previous week, and was keeping her word. It was an olive branch. Whether or not Eddie's twocing counted as 'involvement in motorsport', I wasn't sure, but it had to be worth a shot, didn't it, if only AD would give him Willowmede's backing? And surely he'd do that?

Later on in school, I'd never seen Eddie so excited. He was almost smiling.

'Do you think I could?' he asked.

'Yeah,' I said airily, like I knew the first thing about it. 'You'd be a natural! Go and find AD, and tell him Willowmede have *got* to support you, if the A Club means anything. And remember me when you're pulling ten million a year.'

'Are you going to have a go?' he asked. Wasn't that sweet of him! In Eddie's slightly reptilian way...

'Not me!' I said. 'This is your thing, Eddie. Just for you.'

'Oh,' he said, and looked a bit disappointed. Eddie's ambitions obviously included the car *and* the girl.

With me in school I had a list of things and people to be fixed for the SuperShow. First up was Everard.

Willowmede's revered music supremo was running her bony fingers up and down the big piano in the music room during the few minutes at the end of the lunch hour, glasses steamed up and bouncing on her nose while she gave the keys a good hiding. She's a star on the old joanna, I'll give her that, but Miss Everard's playing is always more Sylvester Stallone than Johnny Depp. It's like she's got a score to settle with the strings. And isn't that a good pun, though I say it myself!

I explained what I was after, as gooily as I knew how... was sure AD and Big Ben would be *sooo* grateful for the presence of the

County Youth Choir, blah blah... good cause, disabled children, blah blah... sorry for last-minute panic, grovel, grovel... while Everard more or less completely ignored me.

Her eyebrows stayed knitted. Her attention stayed glued to the music on the piano in front of her, like it was so much more important and valuable than I was. She licked her thin lips, relishing the moment.

'Out of the question, I'm afraid,' she finally announced smugly, when I'd finished licking the last bit of polish off her smelly shoes. 'Far too late in the day. And at Christmas, too. Our busiest time. Perhaps I need to explain that to Dr Dickson himself, although I'd have thought he'd have known.'

Finally, she turned her gorgon gaze on me. Her eyes were grey and hard behind the specs. 'And perhaps you could tell me, Abigail, why I should do anything for you, when you've so singularly failed to support the County Youth Choir this term? Doesn't it take two to tango?'

Well, that was telling me! I didn't know whether to laugh or throttle her. The picture of me tangoing with Everard was a definite don't-go-there. But on the other hand, I was stunned by the mind-numbing arrogance of the woman, like she was the centre of the whole universe. I briefly contemplated bringing the piano lid down on her fingers and ending two brilliant careers (hers and mine!), but instead went for the soft option.

'Well, maybe you could think if there's the slightest possibility, and let me know by Wednesday,' I said lamely.

'There isn't, and so I won't need to, will I? Perhaps in a similar spirit you can tell me if there's the slightest possibility of your co-operation next term too, at your earliest convenience. But now, Abigail, if you'll excuse me, I have some practice to do...' she said, and returned to give the piano another burst of semi-automatic fire from both barrels.

'Silly cow,' said Char, when I told her. 'Better off without the mangy choir. Tell her to stuff it up her Mozart!'

And we giggled, like you do, but me with a slight sinking feeling, because the next person on my list was Ciarán, and I hadn't seen much of her over the last three weeks either. Well, not since the festival really.

Ciarán and Madeleine were in the dance school's office, having a cup of coffee and a secret ciggy between classes when I arrived at ten to six. How can *dancers* do that? Ciarán tried half-heartedly to hide hers, dangling it guiltily down her side at the risk of a scorch mark on her leotard. Maddie took a brazen drag on her cigarette, inhaling big time and narrowing her eyes to show how grown-up she was, like I'd be remotely impressed.

'Hello, stranger!' Ciarán cried sarcastically. 'We don't see you up this way much these days.'

'Schoolwork,' I said, frowning. And then with an air of mystery, 'Hassle at home... you know...'

'Really?' said Ciarán, hoping for some juicy bits.

'Ciarán, can I ask you a favour?...'

The two of them didn't quite do an Everard on me. They were more into playing hard to get. It was all, *'I don't know about that...what do you reckon, Maddie?... bit short notice, isn't it?... bad time of year... lot of people off sick... have we got time to let people know?... cat's had kittens... got to paint the bathroom... must wash my hair tonight...'* And then Ciarán came straight out with it.

'OK, what's in it for us?'

Don't these people just take your breath away! I told her. Good publicity. A write-up in the paper. Maybe even a spot on local telly! She thought about it for approx. one nanosecond.

'All right. We'll do it. What did you have in mind?'

I told her. Some ensemble jazz numbers to top and tail the two halves of the show. Nothing clever. Rerun stuff they'd done at the festival with the seniors. And something pretty somewhere in the middle.

'Like an old-fashioned variety show, you mean?' Ciarán said. The cigarette was back out in the open now. She was almost getting excited. 'Who else is on the bill, then?'

I told her.

'*Bobby Kennedy?* Oh, he's gorgeous! I like him, don't you, Mad?'

Maddie pulled a 'not likely' face.

'Yeah, well, maybe a bit old for you. But he could sing a duet with me, any time…'

In Ciarán's case, Bobby Kennedy's appearance in SuperShow was definitely the clincher. Don't think it'd have worked with Everard, but I never got that far, did I?

I'm warming to Sally. She's OK. It seems like she's got a bizarre home life to cope with too, which she does with a cheerful good grace. My dad has his faults, but at least I don't have to live with a celeb. Particularly one who calls me 'babes'! Ugh! You know they talk about blokes having 'trophy' girlfriends (horrible expression!), usually meaning big hair, big boobs, small brain? Well, watching Sally with Bobby the other night, it seemed like he wanted her to be his pink'n'fluffy trophy daughter. Which she is so not! She's nice and normal, and down to earth, even about him.

The way the A Club had decided to deal with *Adrenalin Rush* was to audition them. Slightly cheeky, but there you are. Tuesday evening (the band's usual practice night) in the college hall was the designated time and place.

'My dad's not doing much at the moment,' Sally had said. 'He could come and take a look if you want a professional opinion. He can do something useful for a change, instead of hanging about the house all the time.'

Which was an interesting take on the life of a rock star!

I told Pete this on Tuesday morning, and he nearly fell into his cornflakes. He *pretends* to think Bobby Kennedy is back there roaming prehistory with the diplodocus and the sabre-toothed tiger, but secretly you can see he's dead impressed I'm hanging with the daughter of the lead singer in *Wasted*.

When it came to the evening audition, I have to say I wasn't as totally embarrassed as I thought I might be. Pete's singing still sounded like an impression of a chicken in the last seconds of its life, but the rest of the band weren't bad. And on closer inspection, even Pete's guitar playing had improved. I'm sure I spotted a fourth chord in there somewhere.

Bobby was quite into it, in a middle-aged man trying to get down with the yoof kind of way. A couple of times when they finished a song he went 'Yeah', and clapped and whooped. The rest of us – Char, Drew, Em, Sally and me – exchanged glances with each other during this distressing display of uncool, but Bobby seemed blissfully unaware. And when the band took a break after twenty minutes of ear-exploding grunge, he said, 'Great. I think you boys are fabulous. Maybe we could, like, do a couple of numbers together? If the folks here agree?'

We nodded.

'Do you guys know any *Wasted* tracks? Like maybe, "Saturday Night Drunk" or "Let Me Out of Here"?'

Charlie the drummer and Gus the lead guitarist shyly admitted they did. Pete looked doubtful. Char opened her mouth, perhaps to say that this wasn't the kind of show for a song with a title like 'Saturday Night Drunk', but it was too late. Bobby had grabbed a mike, and was teaching the band what they didn't know.

'Time to go,' said Sally, as Bobby started bellowing the words of the chorus:

Rock'n'roll sweetsoul,
Reggae or funk
Really don't care when
I'm Saturday night drunk…

'Have they passed the audition?' I asked Char. She shrugged.

'Don't ask me,' she shrugged. 'I'm no Sharon Osbourne.'

'But you are the producer,' Em pointed out.

'Do you really think we could stop them now?' Drew shouted as the band wobbled into life, and Bobby's rasping voice filled the hall, almost drowning out the backing.

'By the way,' Char said at the college front door, where the sound of *Adrenalin Rush featuring Bobby Kennedy* had faded to a distant roar, 'Tyler says he's up for it.'

'I expect he is. But what about the show?' grumbled Drew.

'And do we get to audition *him*?' asked Em.

'Why not? If you want…' was Char's answer, but with eight days to curtain-up, she knew we were running out of time for any of that.

'You're absolutely sure he means it, and he's not going to turn the whole thing into a gangsta riot?' I said.

Char turned and looked at me with hard eyes.

'It's an offer of help. You're the Christian, Abs. What would Jesus have done?'

Who did she think she was? Jana? Getouttahere!

'Two things,' Char said to me on Wednesday. 'One is, how do we compère the whole thing, 'cos I don't fancy doing it, do you? It ought to be someone with authority, don't you think? I mean, a grown-up. Just in case… you know… there *was* any bother…'

'I thought you said there was no chance of gangsta rioting…'

'Yes. But just to cover everyone's backs…'

'Why don't we let AD sort that one out?'

'Good idea!'

'And the other thing?'

'SuperShow's not very Christmassy yet, is it? What do you reckon about your church choir, since Everard's so in a sulk? Just a couple of carols at the end. You know, in their robes and that… It'd be nice!'

'Yeah, and then they could do a Christmas rap along with Tyler…'

'Ha ha, very funny. Seriously. What are the chances of them singing?'

'Seriously? Haven't a clue. I suppose I could ask.'

Later on in the day, Char and I ran into AD and asked him how he felt about being a compère. He went slightly odd on us, all shy and secretive.

'Funny you should mention that,' he murmured. 'Sandy Johnson and I could probably do it between us. We were talking about it the other day. If you didn't mind two oldies sticking their oars in? We'll find some way of disguising ourselves…'

No, we said, we didn't mind. It'd be a weight off our brains. Really.

Oh God, they probably see themselves as Ant and Dec, I thought. This might be a really gross idea!

He tapped his nose. 'I'll say no more. Just leave it with us. By the way,' he added, 'If this all turns out as well as I'm sure it will…'

Same old AD schmooze…

'… It's going to be very helpful to Willowmede right now. It's been a tough term for the school… the building work, odd problems with the press… you know! We all could do with a bit of success to keep the critics at bay. After all, there are careers on the line here – ours as well as yours!'

What was he going on about? Sometimes AD makes no sense at all. *Here we go again,* I thought. *Say it after me, Adrian. Schools are for kids. Not teachers. Not politicians. Not the Logic Solutions of this world. Aaargh!*

'I get the willies just thinking about the actual night of SuperShow,' said Char, when AD had slid away on his oily slick. 'Suppose no one turns up?'

'Well, there's the special needs kids themselves,' I answered, trying to convince myself. 'And their parents. And think of the number of people we're putting onstage. If everyone sells one ticket, that's probably a full hall already. All without Rosie putting anything in the *Examiner.*'

'All right, I'll shut up,' Char replied. 'You're right. It's a no-brainer. We'll run our own race, and not worry about the rest. Talking about worries, are Drew and Eddie up to speed on light and sound?'

I'd talked technical turkey with Drew earlier. Actually, I'd been unable to avoid it. I'd got cornered, and now knew more than I wanted to.

'In seventh heaven,' I could answer quite genuinely. 'Rambling on in a foreign language about Fresnels and kilowatts, whatever they are. Apparently they've got Lambo involved…'

Mr Lambert. Physics teacher. Big beard and big BO and frankly not my cup of tea.

'… According to Drew, Lambo was a roadie before he went to uni. Now he's wetting himself at the thought of working with Bobby Kennedy. Like most of the rest of the world seems to be!'

'Aren't they just! Do you get it?'

'Can't be Bobby's looks.'

'Or his intelligent conversation…'

'Or his good taste…'

'Must be the size of his…'

'Bank balance!' I finished decisively.

Thursday and Friday were bad days. The thing with Mum and Dad: it's all very peculiar. Some days I've been able to push it right out of the way, and get on with living my life – SuperShow or school or dealing with Rosie or whatever. Other times, I've obsessed endlessly about the Goodenough future, getting used to the idea that some day soon they're going to tell me they're splitting and that will be that, and I'll have to cope with living… well, where? I can't imagine our house without either of them. Or without me. Days like that, I've probably been horrible to know. So that'll have been Thursday and Friday then. Black dog time.

Saturday afternoon, the family were at it again.

'I left some papers on the kitchen table. Have you tidied them up?' Dad asked Mum accusingly. It didn't seem like a big deal to me, but Mum took off like a rocket.

'I haven't touched any of your papers. And anyway, it would serve you right for leaving them lying around. I'm fed up with clearing up after your mess, David. You're worse than the children…'

Gee, thanks, Mum.

Now, what she said to Dad doesn't look much on paper, does it? Spoken with a smile, it mightn't have meant anything at all. But said like Mum actually did, it seemed just then like it meant the whole world, or the end of it. She began to stomp around as she sounded off, banging pans and dishes, slamming cupboard doors. And then suddenly, as she was trying to wedge it where it belonged on the shelves by the fridge, Mum's favourite willow pattern serving dish slipped from her wet hands because she was in such a paddy, and the wretched thing spiralled to the floor and smashed into a thousand pieces. There was a pin-drop slo-mo interval while we all looked stupidly at the broken blue and white remains before Mum's face screwed up into tears, shouting at Dad, 'Now look what you've made me do!' and then there she was down on the floor, cradling pieces of fake Japanese pottery like they'd been worth a jackpot lottery ticket, and sobbing her heart out.

Well, that was it! I suppose it was about time for the dam to burst. Miracle it had stayed in one piece that long!

'Look, you two,' I shouted. 'I've just about had enough of this. I can't bear it any longer. If you're simply staying together for my sake, well, really, I wish you wouldn't. Don't you think it would all be so much better if you were honest and came out into the open, and stopped pretending? Because this is no good for anyone, is it? Not for me, or for you. Just get your stupid divorce and then I can get on with the rest of my life!' And of course I started blubbing too.

Well, that certainly focused their attention!

Mum immediately stopped crying, and sat back on her haunches, wiping her eyes, absolutely poleaxed. Dad went white, and sat down on a chair for support, looking as guilty as hell.

'Divorce, Abi darling?' he said to me, doing a good impression of being completely mystified. 'What on earth are you talking about? No one's getting divorced. Whatever made you think that?'

'All the rows. The constant bickering,' I shouted. 'Do you realize what you've been like to live with these last few weeks? And you just expect me to get on with things and ignore it all? Like there's no stress in *my* life! School going bonkers. Friends falling apart. And there isn't an adult anywhere you can count on to behave properly. Just imagine if I'd gone on the way you guys have. *You* wouldn't have put up with it for two minutes...'

More tears. Hair-twisting. Dramatic gestures. Oh yes, I'm a Goodenough through and through.

'We *have* been under a bit of stress…' Mum said quietly.

'You don't say!' By now I'd gone into a big-time self-righteous strop. I never saw what was coming next. But how could I have been so thick?

'You might want to sit down, Abi, love…'

'We've got some different kind of news for you…'

'What your mother's trying to say is…'

'Abi, I'm pregnant!'

So, correction, that's sex at least *five* times. And at their age, too. Disgusting? I think so. And not very considerate, either.

Blog the Fifteenth
18 December

Last Christmas there was an enormous fuss in the city with some of the council bigwigs wanting to take the Christ bit out of Christmas, and Muslims and Hindus as well as Christians telling them where to get off because nobody else was upset by Bethlehem, wise men and peace on earth, thank you very much. So instead of last year's non-denominational angels and Christmas trees, this year the Christmas lights swinging between the lamp posts are mostly baby Jesuses. As if I needed a reminder about babies right now!

At a stroke my inheritance is down from a fourth of the Goodenough estate to a fifth, there'll be nappies on every radiator, my friends are going to go all gooey/unable to talk about anything else – I can already see Em now! – and life is going to be generally turned upside down. Already I feel jealous of my new brother or sister. (Which do I think it's going to be? By the trouble it's caused already, I reckon it must be a bloke baby.)

And all this, it turns out, was what was worrying M & D over the past month or so. Apparently, they'd seriously been considering Mum having a termination, because they didn't think any of us, me included, could cope. Pity you didn't let me in the loop, guys! Instead, there I was, left dangling like a Christmas decoration.

Abortion seems a dumb idea to me, 99% of the time. Don't you think they'd have been able to make out a good case for Jesus – teen mother, ancient dad likely to have a heart attack any moment, no readies and dodgy digs – and then where would we have been? Mind you, I do wonder what Jesus would have made of twenty-first century Christmas in Leicester. I can just imagine: *'You what? Come on, folks, let's get real! I do these miracles. I die like that. I rise again, and you want to make all that noise about the stable stuff? Priorities, guys, priorities!'*

Anyway. No divorce. No termination. Instead, it's six months contemplating a happy event, and then my GCSE years hampered by sleepless nights before a Terrible Toddler tears up the house while I try to do my A levels. Excellent!

I am just not a baby person. The whole thing seems yucky, beginning to end. Yucky, but as things stand, strangely necessary. You wonder why God couldn't have found a better way. And to think there are people my age getting pregnant! At least from now on I'll know what's going on if Mum (or Dad!) starts throwing crockery.

I haven't told anyone about the Goodenough population explosion. Apart from anything else, there hasn't been the time. We Willowmeders have all been in hyperdrive. The school's gone large on 'practising for examinations', so the keen-type teachers have been throwing humungous end-of-term tests at us. I tried Penny out with, 'You don't really want to do this, do you, sir? Think of all that marking!' but he smiled his crocodile smile and, licking his lips, answered, 'But I *like* marking, Abigail. One of the great satisfactions of life! To sit in judgment on others, free from responsibility! As you may one day find out...'

The idiot man still really cherishes the hope I might allow myself to be locked into doing French A level with him for two whole years! Get a life! And I really object to his snidey insinuation I could end up a teacher! There are only a few million jobs I'd do first, like washing plates at a fast food outlet, or cleaning the city centre toilets.

So what with tests, churchy Christmas things, fitting in some Christmas shopping, *and* getting ready for SuperShow, this has definitely been the end-of-term with more. No room for extras. Which is why when Eddie buttonholed me on Tuesday morning, I wasn't quickly into his thinking zone.

'I've had another letter,' he gibbered.

'Yeah, good!' I said, trying to ignore him and stuff my head with amazing facts for regurgitation in the Big History Test five minutes later.

'Leicester Raceway. The karting geezers!' Eddie was almost hyperventilating.

'Right! Great!' I said, summoning up enthusiasm from a distant region of my cranium at about one and a half on a scale of ten.

'They want me to go along on Thursday night for that speed trial.'

'Fantastic…' The bell was about to go. If only I could just cram in a last few, undoubtedly vital details into my head…

'Will you come with me?'

Duh! There are still occasionally moments like this with Eddie, when he looks at me pleadingly, hopefully, from underneath the hair, like I might morph into the girl of his dreams.

'Bad moment, Eddie. I've got a trial of my own, like… History?'

He looked crestfallen. And of course, straight away I felt like a rat. It *was* good news, after all.

'Well, maybe *everyone* would like to come? Let's make it an A Club night out!' I said, trying desperately to save myself by dumping on other people.

Funnily enough, in the end, five of us *did* pitch up on Thursday night for Eddie's karting debut. Only Drew missed out.

'Lambo needs me for some help with wiring,' he said, making like we were all deserting our posts because we were spending time on something not immediately connected with SuperShow. 'Thursday at eight is zero hour minus forty-eight and counting. Or if you're counting the dress rehearsal, zero hour minus forty-two…'

(We'd set up a rehearsal for Saturday afternoon, so that everyone would at least know how to get on and off stage at the right time. Drew's a party-pooper. But I suppose someone had to do the worrying for the rest of us. Manic obsessives have their uses.)

'… But don't you worry your little heads. You just all go off and enjoy yourselves.'

So we did. AD too, because someone official from Eddie's 'sponsor', i.e. Willowmede, had to be there.

As an evening's entertainment, it wasn't absolutely fun-on-a-stick, but it wasn't the pits (ha ha) either. However, it *was* freezing cold, because all we were doing was standing about watching while various kids and karts wobbled and whizzed round the little stadium in between the piles of tyres and gravel traps. Char, bless her, had brought a large thermos of coffee, so at least we could swap a few germs and have the occasional swig of something warm.

The chap on the gate didn't want to let us all in at first, and AD had to do a bit of a number on him. I don't think they're used to spectators on a Thursday night. But when the bloke saw we weren't going to break up the joint, he became quite friendly, and told us his name was Mick. Mick watched Eddie as he went round a few times, going gently at first, and then noticeably quicker as his confidence improved.

'That your mate, then?' he asked.

'Yeah,' we said casually, like we did this all the time.

'He's got it,' Mick said, nodding his head approvingly. 'Natural speed, like!'

Suddenly Eddie hurtled into a corner far too fast, and for a bad moment looked like he'd completely lost control of his 'natural speed' as he plunged towards a tyre wall. At the last second, with Eddie's hands a blur on the tiny steering wheel, the kart lurched left and right, and he was through the corner and on to the next.

Mick laughed. 'Blimey,' he said. 'That's good. Very good. You say he's never been on a track before?'

We confirmed that he hadn't. We didn't bother telling him about Eddie's wider driving experience.

When he'd had his fifteen minutes of fame, and joined us by the ramshackle group of huts which were the Leicester Raceway's HQ, Eddie was somewhere out beyond Pluto. We told him he'd been wicked, and watched him grow a few inches.

'That... was... [*expletive deleted*] brilliant!' he puffed. 'Oh, sorry, sir! Didn't see you!' You'd have thought Eddie had run a marathon, he was that out of breath.

'Have you won the scholarship?' asked Syl.

'They say they'll let me know. By Saturday.'

Early on SuperShow day, Saturday morning, while I was still lying in bed, Mum shouted up the stairs that Sally was on the phone. I picked up her call with a sinking feeling. All along I'd had a sneaking idea the thing with Bobby Kennedy was far too good to be true.

'It's Dad,' she said. Well, what a surprise! Being Sally, I couldn't tell if she was as cross with him as I was. Rain or shine, Sally seems to take everything just the same. 'He's stuck in an airport somewhere in Glasgow because of fog. Says there's no way he'll make it to the rehearsal. And at this rate he's not sure about tonight either.'

'But it's only nine in the morning,' I moaned at her. 'That gives him *eleven* hours to get to Leicester. He could *walk* it in that time. And anyway, why are you telling me, Sally? Char's the one who needs to know: she's the producer!'

'I know, I know,' Sally said defensively. 'Dad's always like this. You know I said about him being home for Christmas. Well, it looks as if that's blown out now as well. You can never count on him for anything. And I can't get hold of Char. Her mobile's been switched off all morning.'

'OK... Well, try her landline then...'

And I gave Sally the number at Thornton Bramleigh, telling her to call me back if she had no luck. Why can't *anybody* I know organize a binge in a brewery?

Ten minutes later, Sally called again. No Char, no anyone at Thornton.

'Well, there's nothing we can do,' I said, trying my hardest to be practical, while mentally sticking pins in effigies of AD, Bobby Kennedy and Char. 'We'll just have to manage the best we can this afternoon. It probably won't be the last thing to go wrong!'

How much of a fortune-teller am I?

When I arrived at the school theatre at one fifteen, a bit earlier than I'd planned because Char had gone AWOL (there *still* wasn't any reply from her numbers), it had that strange, dead, depressing feeling some buildings have when they're empty. Then the sound of a spanner hitting metal echoed around the ceiling, and looking up, I saw Drew, a monkey in his tree, squatting high on one of the walkways which stretched over the auditorium in front of the stage.

'Wotcher, Abs,' he hollered. 'Just fixing the last couple of lamps. I'll be down in a mo!'

'Anybody else here?' I shouted into the rafters.

'All the gear for the bands came in this morning,' he said.

'Bands?' I queried. 'Plural? Pete's lot are the only band I know of.'

'Well, them and Tyler's crew,' he said, gesturing towards the stage. On it was assembled a mountain of speakers and bits of various drum kits. It looked like Coldplay were setting up to play Wembley.

Gradually people began to arrive, mostly Ciarán's dancers, then Sylvester and his uncle carrying armfuls of props they wanted to add to the rubbish on the stage, then a couple of *Adrenalin Rush* looking like they'd left all their adrenalin in a club somewhere at four the previous morning, and just after *them* a bunch of people I didn't know at all.

'We're with Tyler, man, innit?' suggested a massively overweight boy with a much too small Chicago White Sox baseball cap.

'All of you?'

'Right!'

There were a dozen people tagging along with him, all now lolling about on the front seats, comparing trainers for size, make and general phatitude.

'And Tyler?'

'He's cool!'

No doubt. But not present, which was more to the point.

It was five to two. Mind you, we were still missing one producer too, weren't we? Where *was* Char? Knots of performers had spread themselves around the auditorium, eyeing each other's cliques nervously, not knowing who should organize whom.

Tyler arrived last, at about two fifteen, roughly the same time as Eddie Finn, swaggering in and swapping complicated hand-grabs with his crew. Eddie looked as miserable as sin. Still no Char.

Ciarán's sidekick Maddie wandered wetly up to me.

'Ciarán says she's very sorry but she's done her back, and can't get out of bed. She's says she's gutted, and I'm to be in charge. Ooh, and could you get her Bobby Kennedy's autograph?'

Deep joy. AD sauntered past.

'Don't you think we should get going, Abi?' he whispered.

'Char's not here,' I said.

'Well, I think you'll just have to start without her. Do you want me to rally the troops?'

'No... no,' I replied, heart pounding. 'It's got to be down to us, hasn't it? Leave it to me.'

And wishing I'd never ever got myself involved, I took a deep breath and yelled at the assembled company, speaking so fast even *I* didn't understand me.

'Listen, please. We're going to run through the show, starting at three o'clock, and not a minute later. So by then everything needs to be in the right place and ready to go. That means all the band equipment, all the props, all the people. Got that? And you'll need a running order...' At least we had those, courtesy of AD and the staff reprographic room:

SUPERSHOW
The running order

IMPORTANT

Do not lose this. Do not exceed UR time. Do what Em tells U!

First Half   8.00 p.m.

Dancers (1)   3 mins

Adrenalin Rush   15 mins

Syl's Magic World (1)   5 mins

FF Crew (Tyler)   15 mins

Dancers (2)   3 mins

+ Dickson & Johnson to fill = 5 mins

Second Half   9.15 p.m.

Dancers (3)   3 mins

Syl's Magic World (2)   5 mins

Abi's spot   5 mins

Bobby Kennedy   20 mins

+ Adrenalin Rush   10 mins

St. Michael's choir   15 mins

+ Dickson & Johnson to fill = 5 mins

Even before the walk-through there were problems and aggro.

Like, there wasn't room for two drum kits on stage, Em reported, not with everything else.

'Respect, man,' said Tyler's drummer, meaning the opposite, 'but no way is I using a pile of old tin cans like that!' He was pointing at *Adrenalin Rush*'s drums.

'What you trying to say? You're too good for them, or something?'

'You heard them, man! They ain't tuned or nothin'! Bunch of tin cans would do better!'

'...And how are the dancers supposed to work with all that rubbish cluttering up the stage, anyway?' Maddie was moaning. 'It'll have to be moved. I can't tell Ciarán one of the dancers done themselves a mischief, can I?'

'...That's it, man. I'm out of here. I ain't being talked to like that...' Tyler's drummer was on his high horse (or should that be his hi-hat!), feeling well disrespected.

And so on. I diverted AD into dealing with Tyler and *Adrenalin Rush*, while I sorted out Maddie.

Eventually, under pressure, *Adrenalin*'s drummer grudgingly admitted Tyler's kit was better than his. Em persuaded the musicians to give Maddie another ten centimetres of space. No one took their guitar or tutu home in a sulk. But it was a close thing.

And then, finally, at five to three, Char finally waltzed in, apparently completely unfazed by her later than late arrival.

'Where have you *been*?' I hissed furiously.

'I'm sooo sorry, Abs. Couldn't help it. I'll tell you all about it later. How are we doing?'

'OK. Just about. No thanks to you.'

Everyone walked uncertainly through the rehearsal. AD and Sandy gibbered between acts.

'They're not very funny,' Char complained.

'*You* tell them, then!' I snorted.

'We'll just mark it for now,' Sandy shouted down, as if he'd heard us. 'It'll be all right on the night.'

As for the rest, the sound was awful, the lights were on when they should have been off, and off when they should have been on, *Adrenalin Rush* fell apart, the dancers fell over, Syl and his uncle looked like they'd die a death because none of their tricks would work, I danced like my feet were tied together, the choir weren't going to be there till the evening anyway, star attraction Bobby Kennedy probably wasn't going to make it at all, and Tyler…

Well, surprise, surprise, Tyler and his crew were *really* bootyliciously excellent. There was a very loud guitarist and a drummer plus a wacky-looking kid in dreads scratching on a turntable, and a girl dancer out front gyrating like crazy beside Tyler and his sidekick. Who both rapped like they totally meant it, blowing everyone away by even being laugh-out-loud funny a couple of times. When they finished their third and last number, the rest of the performers erupted in spontaneous applause, and Tyler bowed stiffly to his new fanbase.

'Respec' to the bredren,' he said, and jumped off the stage, to whoops and hollers from his own crowd of supporters.

Just then Eddie slouched past, hands in pockets, looking dejected.

'What's up, Ed?' I asked.

'Ain't heard nothin' from the karting place,' he grumbled.

'Oh,' I said, genuinely disappointed for him. 'That's a shame. Don't give up, Eddie. You were fantastic. I'm sure they'll call you.'

'Yeah! To tell me to get lost, most like!' Eddie mooched off sadly.

Bad rehearsal, great show. Well, that's what Ciarán's dinned into me since I was about nine. And that's what I told the rest of the A Club at the rehearsal post-mortem, though no one looked convinced. I didn't really believe it myself.

'We've just got to hold our nerve,' I encouraged, still doing Char's job for her. 'All for one, and one for all. Live the dream!'

'Who are you kidding?' scoffed Drew. 'It's gonna be pants, and you know it!'

'It will so not!' I replied. 'You'll see! Any news about Bobby yet?'

Sally shrugged. 'Search me!' she muttered grimly. Actually, I felt sorry for her. She probably wanted to show off her dad to everyone, and he was letting her down.

'Well, we won't panic until we know we have to,' I said, crossing my fingers and simultaneously asking God if he'd mind just this once bending the rules of time and space, and delivering Bobby Kennedy before it was too late.

And that was it. Nothing more I did now would make a difference as to whether SuperShow stunk or stonked, so I had Pete drive me home to shower and change, thinking, *Why, oh why, did we agree to this embarrassment? Never again. Next term, it's the easy way out for me every time!*

When we returned to the theatre, me telling myself that at least this torment would all be over in another three hours or so, Eddie Finn was waiting. He was positively jubilant.

'I done it,' he was shouting. 'I got it. I done it!'

'The karting scholarship?'

'Yeah. They texted me an hour ago. Two sessions a week, starting January.'

Eddie was bopping up and down so convincingly he was in danger of being promoted from assistant sound engineer to star attraction. Maybe our luck was changing, and it was a good omen for the evening.

In the green room behind the stage, Char was fidgeting.

'I feel like a spare part,' she worried. 'Isn't there anything I can do?'

'Not now,' I said. 'Too late for that. Prayer for a miracle would be good. By the way, why *were* you so late this afternoon?'

Char was still aggravatingly nonchalant. 'Oh yeah, sorry! Mum and Dad are trying to get back together again. We all kind of went off to a hotel for the night to talk about it. Dad's idea at the last moment. I should have told you, I know!'

'We all kind of went off to a hotel!' Oh, puh-lease!

'That's brilliant news,' I said, not knowing whether to hug or slap her. 'Amazing! But yes, you should have told us. It was dead irresponsible, Char! Really it was.'

She coloured up.

'I don't know what came over me,' she said. 'SuperShow just went, like, completely out of my head. It didn't seem to matter. Not while we were away. We were in our own little bubble. I knew you'd all cope without me. I didn't think Mum and Dad could.'

Supposing it had been me? I thought. *Wouldn't I have felt the same?* No, I'd have picked up the phone.

I wandered round to the front of the theatre. Maybe no one was going to turn up and we could all go home. But no, people were streaming in. Kids in wheelchairs with carers and friends. Teachers from the school. The Mayor with his jangling gold chain. A few other suits. The MD of Logic Solutions. Big Ben schmoozing everyone. Oh, and there were my parents, waving at me. I made a sharp exit.

Back in the green room, the hands of the clock moved towards eight and show time. No Bobby Kennedy.

'OK,' I said to Char and Em. *'Now* we panic. What do we do?'

'Not many options, are there?' Em observed.

'Few more carols?' Char suggested.

'Yeah, and either Tyler or Adrenalin Rush will have to play a second set.'

I pulled a face. 'Perhaps we should see how they go down with the punters in the first half? No point in flogging a dead horse!'

'*You* could sing something,' Em said. 'You've got an amazing voice. I don't think you know how good it is!'

Wasn't that a lovely thing to say? I had my friend back. We'd worked together brilliantly over the last week or so. Just like old times.

'Well, let's hope it doesn't come to that,' I said. 'We don't want to scrape the bottom of the barrel, do we?'

'Scraping the bottom of the barrel would be, like, *me* standing up and singing,' said Em, cackling. 'As you well know. And then we'd have to give people their money back.'

The door of the green room opened, and two enormous women with outrageous rouged make-up strode in, adjusting their vast bosoms vulgarly as they came. Two very ugly sisters. AD and Sandy Johnson. Now we understood the secrecy.

'Ready for the off, everybody?' asked what was probably Sandy Johnson from somewhere deep inside a covering of corset. He'd acquired a new voice, straight off the set of Corrie. 'Hi! I'm Dora. This one's Beat. She's feeling a bit dead, aren't you, Beat?' We groaned and fell about appropriately.

AD's accent was rather worse than Sandy's. It hovered between Sydney, Australia, and Barnsley, England. 'Come on, Dora dear,' he trumpeted, 'let's go and dip our sticks in the sump of the audience's oil of compassion.'

And hoisting their 46 DD's back into position, they strode onstage. This was high risk, high camp. There might shortly be two vacancies on Willowmede's teaching staff next term if Big Ben didn't see the joke! I couldn't quite believe greasy but cool AD had allowed the old ham Sandy Johnson to put him up to it.

The first half was OK. Tyler was good, but this wasn't his audience. The people in the seats were more Old Skool than phat and funky. A few fingers went in ears during *Adrenalin Rush*'s set, but some of the wheelchairs were rocking. Syl and his uncle were excellent. Maybe we should have given them more space. This time all the tricks worked, and you could see the delight on the kids' faces. And Maddie was very pleased with her performance – I mean, with her *dancers'* performance.

'You were *so* brilliant,' she gushed to them at the interval. 'Just wait till I tell Ciarán how good you were without her!'

AD and Sandy were *very* funny: they just had to walk onstage and look at each other for the audience to start cracking up, particularly those who twigged who they were.

'Living with Beat is just like a fairy tale,' began Sandy, aka Dora. 'Grimm…'

I sneaked a look at Big Ben while his two employees strutted their womanly stuff six feet from where he was sitting on the front row. There was a strange half-smile fixed on his face. He occasionally shifted round on his bottom, to see how other people around him were reacting. He was wondering if he could afford to find this amusing.

Half-time came and the moment of decision. So who was getting to be the substitute Bobby Kennedy?

Syl and his uncle looked dubious about taking a second spot. It wouldn't be them. Tyler was playing the big man, relaxed and generous.

'Let those guys do it,' he said, jerking a thumb at *Adrenalin Rush*. 'They's kickin'. It ain't the same for us wivout our crew. Make a rush for the *Rush*, right?'

'We're cool with that,' said Pete, pretending they weren't wetting themselves at this new opportunity to cause temporary deafness and suffering. 'I could sing those two songs of Bobby Kennedy's… no problem!'

But then, just as if Pete had said '*Shazam*', the door of the green room opened and the long-lost singer himself materialized, not a hair out of place, and even, unless I was very much mistaken, wearing some foundation and a touch of eyeliner. Obviously Char *had* been praying. Oh thank you, God!

'How ya doin'?' he asked no one in particular, putting his guitar case down in a corner.

Up on stage, Bobby was a pro, you've got to give it to him. Just one bloke and a guitar, and yet they were eating out of his hand. Even Big Ben's foot seemed to be twitching. Personally, I think the two songs BK sang with *Adrenalin Rush* were a mistake, but after five minutes of *that* dreadful racket, he clapped off the band and asked for the lights to be turned down. Onstage alone, caught in a single shaft of white light, he sang 'Away in a Manger' so quietly you had to strain to catch the words. Not a dry seat in the house!

The St Michael's choir picked it up from there. The audience sang along tunelessly and happily with 'The First Nowell' and 'Once in Royal David's City', and everyone went home blissed out.

There was a whole lot of hugging going on afterwards. I couldn't avoid Maddie's. I was happy to make up and swap one with Char. Em and I don't hug. Never have. Can't reach! Pete and Tyler were swapping manly footballer's embraces and high fives. Dora and Beat, aka AD and Sandy, were shaking hands. Drew and Eddie had disappeared, just in case.

'Respect, man!' said Tyler. I looked over my shoulder to see who he was talking to.

'No, you. *Lickle* girl!' he said. That twisted grimace on his face was probably a smile. Tyler was sending himself up. 'You! The Abi National girl! I gotta put myself under heavy manners and say sorry for that stuff the other week. I was well out of order, thinking you were stuck up and that. Respect, you're all right, you know. You small but you got da power, and you done real good.'

Well, that smacked my gob, didn't it! 'Thanks,' I said. 'I thought you were great too!'

Well, I did!

'One other t'ing... I know who done your house, right? Wasn't me, but I know who did it. And they swear to me they're gonna return that computer they nicked. OK?'

What was coming next, a proposal of marriage? The Christmas

spirit was definitely breaking out big time.

Char took me to one side and said quietly, 'Thanks for putting up with me this term!'

'Yeah, well, it was nothing. You'd do the same for me.'

'Well, anyway, whatever. Look, I was going to say, can I come to church with you on Christmas Eve? I've got another thank you to say... you know? I mean, it's not fixed – my family stuff. And I don't know if it ever can be. But at least Mum, Dad and me... we'll all be together this Christmas, whatever happens later on...'

Outside the theatre, as people wished each other a Happy Baby Festival under a clear, starry night, who should I bump into but Rosie Pickings, looking very glam. She seemed genuinely pleased to see me.

'Fantastic show,' she smiled. 'Well done you. And I'll tell the *Examiner*'s readers so on Monday. Hope you made some money for a good cause.'

Rosie swivelled and looked all around at the shapes of the academy's half-finished buildings looming out of the dark at us. 'It's a new place, isn't it?' she said. 'Don't recognize most of it. Don't like all of it. But it's better than it was before.' And she tapped off on her high heels towards the car park. Before she disappeared into the night, she turned and shouted, 'Peace!'

Last word

So enough of this soppy goo. Let's do some serious brainwork, guys. What do you reckon then? Like I asked about four months ago, do we make stuff happen, or does it happen to us?

Now I've been thinking about this, and for me, it's a bit of both, though I can't work out what that *means*. Yeah, *we* made SuperShow work, with a bit of luck and help from British Airways. And looking back on when I was feeling my worst this term, there *have* been things I've done to make me feel proud. Being there for Char and Drew. Sorting out Rosie. Keeping Eddie going.

But like Jana said, you can't fix everything. I think I really do know that now. Stuff happens. Mum and Dad didn't mean for Mum to get pregnant. It was just an accident, and goodness knows how a baby's going to change our lives. Right now, it feels like a gigantic leap into the unknown. Will we cope?

And if the village goss is right about Hughesey, what do you say about *that*? What could she have done to avoid what's happening to her? AD's a smarmy oik, but he doesn't deserve for his girlfriend to get cancer. It's frightening. And she's been really nice to us this term.

They were the last people I saw as we were driven away from the theatre after SuperShow. They were standing together by the front entrance to the school and just to one side. He was wrapping her up in his arms, tenderly winding a scarf round her neck, shielding her from the cold. Her head was on his chest. She looked small and vulnerable.

What does the future hold for them in the New Year? Or me, come to that?

THE END